Get ready for
an incredible
adventure . . .

Geronimo Stilton

THE PHOENIX OF DESTINY

AN EPIC KINGDOM OF FANTASY ADVENTURE

Scholastic Inc.

Text by Geronimo Stilton
Original title *Grande Ritorno nel Regno della Fantasia*
Cover by Silvia Fusetti with Gabriele Sina. Illustration of Geronimo Stilton by Silvia Bigolin.

Illustrations by Danilo Barozzi, Silvia Bigolin, Federico Brusco, Carla De Bernardi, Silvia Fusetti, Carolina Livio, Anna Merli, Alessandro Muscillo and Piemme's Archives. Inks by Riccardo Stisti. Color by Christian Aliprandi.
Graphics by Marta Lorini and Chiara Cebraro, with Paolo Zadra and Yuko Egusa.

Special thanks to Kathryn Cristaldi
Translated by Julia Heim
Interior design by Kay Petronio

19 18 17 16 15   20 21 22 23

Printed in China   62
First edition, September 2015

In a land far, far,
far away . . .

In a kingdom of fairies
and giants and dragons . . .

A daring, exciting,
amazing adventure awaits!

Don't be a
'fraidy mouse — read on!

I HAVE A SECRET . . .

H ello, mouse friends! My name is Stilton, *Geronimo Stilton*. Yep, it's really me — your friend from New Mouse City!

You probably already know that I run *The Rodent's Gazette*, the most FAMOUSE newspaper on Mouse Island. But I am more than just a newspaper mouse. Let me tell you some FACTS about myself before we get started!

Let me tell you about myself!

LET ME TELL YOU SOME FACTS ABOUT MYSELF!

Oh, how I like to read!

I am a
SCAREDY-MOUSE!
I'm not sporty or
adventurous at all.

But I still go on
exciting, fur-raising
adventures in a place
called the **KINGDOM
of FANTASY!**

A dragon? Ack!

Now let me begin my **STORY** . . .

The afternoon when everything started, I was at home trying out a new recipe  for enormouse extra-chewy, extra-chocolaty chocolate chip cookies. Yum!

As I prepared the cookie dough, my telephone rang . . .

Ring, ring, riiiinnnnnnngggggg!

I grabbed the phone, still clutching my wooden spoon, which was **dripping** with chocolate. Oops! What a **mess**!

"Stilton, Geronimo Stilton, squeaking!" I snapped.

Geronimo Stilton squeaking!

I heard my grandfather William Shortpaws yelling in the receiver. Rats!

"**GRANDSON!** Remember that you are due to **write** another Kingdom of Fantasy book! It better be an amazing adventure!" he screamed.

Oh, why was he always screaming? I nodded, even though he couldn't see me, and squeaked, "Yes, I know, another fantasy adventure —" but before I could continue, Grandfather interrupted me.

Grandson!

"No, not just another fantasy adventure!" he thundered. "This one needs to be an extra-special book! It needs to be super-adventurous, super-scary, and super-fun! It needs to be epic! Now get started! I'll call you in a few hours to make sure you're not slacking off!"

I sighed and hung up the phone. I knew I had to get to work. Otherwise, Grandfather William would NEVER leave me alone!

Still, I decided a tasty cookie or two might give me inspiration. Ten minutes later . . .

DING!

My cookies were done!

I made myself a cup of tea and put some **warm** cookies on a plate. Then I sat in my favorite pawchair in front of a cozy fire. Ah, how relaxing!

I wasn't really in the **MOOD** to write, but I knew I had to get cracking. Grandfather William would be calling me, demanding to know what my ideas were for the extra-special book.

I took my notebook and my pen and began scribbling away. "Let's see . . . cheese, bananas, toilet paper, **pizza bagels** . . ."

Oops! I was accidentally writing a shopping list!

I refocused, and before I knew it, hours had gone by. As I stared at the **BLAZE** in the fireplace, I noticed something strange. The flames looked like **EYES** in the dark . . .

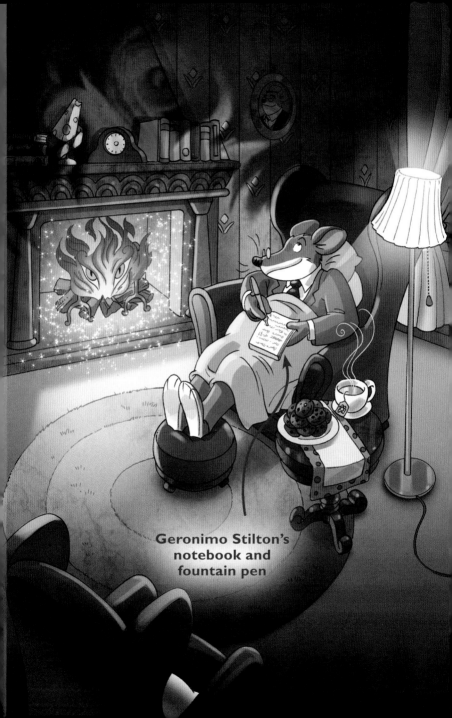

Geronimo Stilton's
notebook and
fountain pen

Suddenly, I realized that those eyes belonged to a fantastical creature . . . the Phoenix of Destiny!

ARE YOU READY FOR ANOTHER ADVENTURE?

The phoenix jumped out of the fireplace, surrounded by a cloud of sparks.

Holey cheese! What was a fantastical creature like the Phoenix of Destiny doing in my living room? I **PINCHED** my fur to make sure I wasn't dreaming.

Ouch!

Ouch!

Nope, I was definitely awake!

I stared at the phoenix. Her beak was the purest gold, her eyes were glittering emerald green, and she had the most amazing

Huh? A phoenix?

thick, **flaming red** feathers.

Yep, the phoenix really was a spectacular bird!

Of course, this wasn't the first time I had seen the phoenix. I had met her during my first trip to the Kingdom of Fantasy. She helped me escape from Cackle, the terrifying queen of the witches! Ack! Talk about a bad memory!

"Ahem — er — hello again. So, what brings you to New Mouse City? Just flying by? Looking for a late-night snack?" I squeaked hopefully. Don't get me wrong; it was great seeing the phoenix, but every time I got one of these visits from someone from the Kingdom of Fantasy, it usually meant I was in for another frightening adventure. Did I mention I'm a scaredy-mouse?

On cue, the bird answered, "Are you ready for another long and scary adventure, Sir Geronimo of Stilton?"

I gulped. "Um, well, you see, I . . ."

The phoenix interrupted me. "You don't have to answer me now, but you do have to come with

Geronimo Stilton

Sir Geronimo of Stilton

me. **SHE** has given an order," the bird chirped.

"**SHE?**" I asked.

"Yes, she. The one and only **Blossom**, the queen of the fairies!" the phoenix proclaimed.

Cheese and crackers! I was a **nervous wreck**, but I could never say no to Queen Blossom. If she needed my help, I was prepared to give it!

Taking a deep breath, I climbed onto the bird's back.

She flapped her wings, then dove into the fireplace, up the chimney, and out into the night sky!

Whew! It was a good thing the phoenix had MAGICAL powers, or I would have become mouse toast!

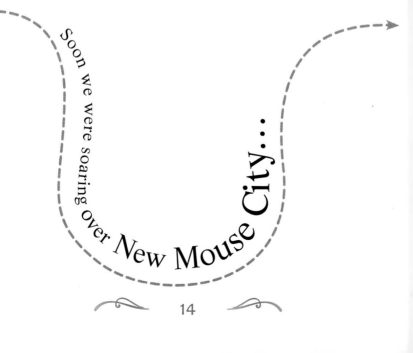

Soon we were soaring over New Mouse City...

MORE DIFFICULT, MORE MYSTERIOUS, MORE DANGEROUS . . .

fter about **three thousand hours** (well, okay, maybe it wasn't that long, but it seemed like forever!), I was able to relax. Did I tell you that I'm afraid of heights?

I peered into the night sky. The moon shone brightly like a ball of mozzarella, and the stars twinkled. Ah, what a beautiful sight!

Just then I thought of something I'd been meaning to ask the phoenix. "I was wondering," I began. "Why did Blossom's call come when I was **awake** this time instead of when I was sleeping?"

The red bird smiled and explained that since I had visited the Kingdom of Fantasy so many times

I was now considered to be a **Gold Standard** Kingdom of Fantasy Traveler. Apparently, that meant that I could go to the kingdom anytime, night or day. Sweet Swiss slices! I felt so **SPECIAL**!

I was still contemplating how special I was when the phoenix interrupted my thoughts. "You should know, Sir Knight," she said, "this time, your trip to the Kingdom of Fantasy will be **MORE** difficult, **MORE** mysterious, **MORE** adventurous, **more** exhausting, and **way, way more** dangerous than ever before."

Hmmm . . . maybe **SPECIAL** wasn't exactly the word I was looking for. No, in fact, now I was feeling totally **TERRIFIED**!

I tried to ask more questions, but the phoenix wouldn't say a peep. We flew on in silence until she whispered, "Be careful, Knight. Lots of things have **CHANGED** in the Kingdom of Fantasy."

I was dying to know more, but in a swirl of bright, shimmering stars . . . we had arrived in the Kingdom of Fantasy! down, down, down we began to spin

THE
KINGDOM
OF
FANTASY

JESS THE JEWELED DRAGONESS

I figured the phoenix would be flying me straight to Blossom's **castle**, but instead she gently deposited me on a cloud. **HUH?**

"Knight, I must leave you," she explained. "I have an urgent appointment with a friend of yours. He needs one of my feathers to finish writing a very important work and, well . . . that's another story. Anyway, I'm going to leave you on this cloud, and you'll be picked up by another fantastical creature."

Another fantastical creature? I blinked. What if

it was **SCARY**? What if it was **mean**? What if it had six heads and they all started yelling at me?

Still, I didn't want the phoenix to think I was a 𝔫𝔢𝔯𝔳𝔬𝔲𝔰 rat, so I just waved good-bye.

"Be careful!" the bird called before she left.

Soon a beautiful dragoness as white as 𝕤𝕟𝕠𝕨 and wearing a **GLITTERING** jewel-studded crown arrived. Her eyes were as **BLUE** as cornflowers, and when she spoke, her voice was as sweet as honey. "Welcome, Knight!" she said.

A minute later, we were flying toward **CRYSTAL CASTLE** ...

This dragon had a car-seat contraption on her back, which was quite **COMFY**. Not that I'm an

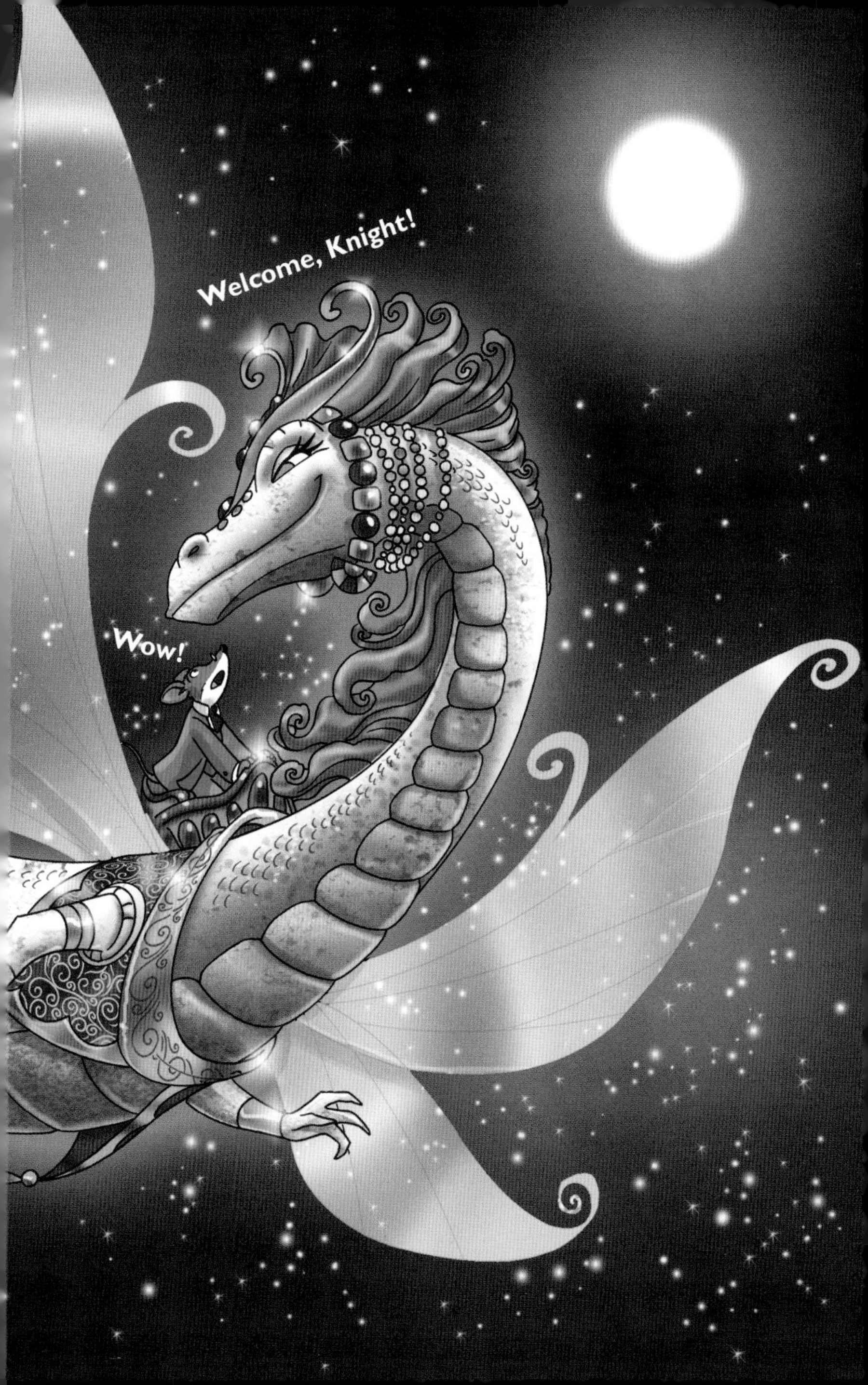
Welcome, Knight!
Wow!

expert on dragon seats, but on my previous trips to the Kingdom of Fantasy I had spent a decent amount of time on the back of my friend the **DRAGON OF THE RAINBOW**. I always felt like I

The Dragon of the Rainbow
Blossom's faithful messenger, he transported Geronimo on his first voyage to the Kingdom of Fantasy. The dragon has golden scales and horns in all the colors of the rainbow. He likes to sing his words instead of speaking them, and he smells like roses!

was going to fly off his back!

As if reading my thoughts, the dragon said, "I know you're used to the DRAGON OF THE RAINBOW, Knight. But allow me to introduce myself. I'm Jess the Jeweled Dragoness. I'm the winner of the Dragon High-Flying Championship, and I specialize in thrilling landings."

High-Flying Champion

Blossom of the Flowers
Queen of the Fairies and Lady of Peace and Happiness. She is sweet, wise, and beautiful. She lives in Crystal Castle.

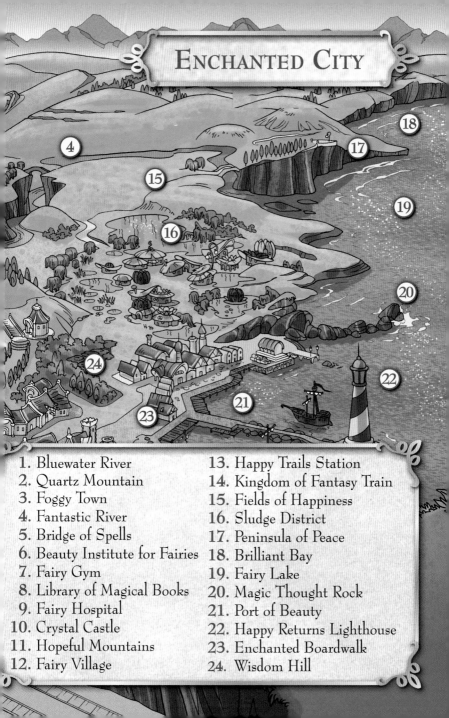

ENCHANTED CITY

1. Bluewater River
2. Quartz Mountain
3. Foggy Town
4. Fantastic River
5. Bridge of Spells
6. Beauty Institute for Fairies
7. Fairy Gym
8. Library of Magical Books
9. Fairy Hospital
10. Crystal Castle
11. Hopeful Mountains
12. Fairy Village
13. Happy Trails Station
14. Kingdom of Fantasy Train
15. Fields of Happiness
16. Sludge District
17. Peninsula of Peace
18. Brilliant Bay
19. Fairy Lake
20. Magic Thought Rock
21. Port of Beauty
22. Happy Returns Lighthouse
23. Enchanted Boardwalk
24. Wisdom Hill

DRAGON LANDING STRIP

Suddenly, Crystal Castle appeared before us, **sparkling** in the bright moonlight like a thousand diamonds.

Jess headed toward the roof of the castle, where I spotted the landing strip. At the center, there was writing in the *Fantasian Alphabet.* Can you translate it?

TO TRANSLATE THE MESSAGE YOURSELF, YOU CAN FIND THE FANTASIAN ALPHABET ON PAGE 575. OR YOU CAN FIND THE MESSAGE IN ENGLISH ON PAGE 576.

Here is Crystal Castle!

A uniformed dragon signaled to us, roaring, "Control Tower to approaching dragoness: Prepare for landing! Reduce your SPEED! Land in the center of the landing strip, and do not breathe FIRE!"

A split second later, Jess began a nightmarish nosedive and a series of twists and turns so terrifying my fur turned a SICKLY shade of GREEN. Great chunks of cheddar!

This way!

No, over here!

Not there, here!

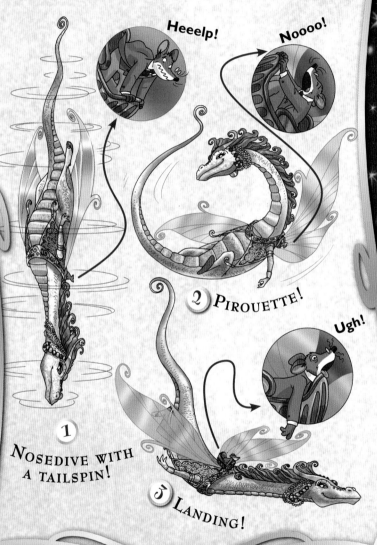

In the end, Jess made a perfect landing.

"**ABSOLUTELY AMAZING!**" roared all the dragons.

Jess **smoothed** her wings and shrugged off the compliments. "Oh, it was nothing. Just a few little **tricks** I picked up at the

DRAGON ACADEMY."

Meanwhile, my stomach was still doing flip-flops. My tail was drooping, and my fur was as **GREEN** as a **lizard**! I knew I suffered

Glub!

from seasickness, but who'd ever heard of **DRAGON-SICKNESS**?!

A FAIRY NAMED NEFARIA

A tall, pale fairy with **fiery** red hair arrived. She had a pointy nose, thin lips, and an evil expression. "I am Nefaria, the new advisor to the queen! Follow me!" she instructed, waving her wand.

So much for small talk!

GIANTS

PIXIES

UNICORNS

Nefaria, the Queen's New Advisor
Daughter of the fairy Hideous (famous for her incomparable ugliness) and the wizard Halfbaked (who specializes in spells that sometimes work and sometimes don't). Nefaria is known to be rotten to the core!

I raced after her through a maze of CRYSTAL halls and stairs and rooms until we reached the Ceremony Room. It was filled with tons of different types of creatures from around the Kingdom of Fantasy!

GNOMES

Fairies

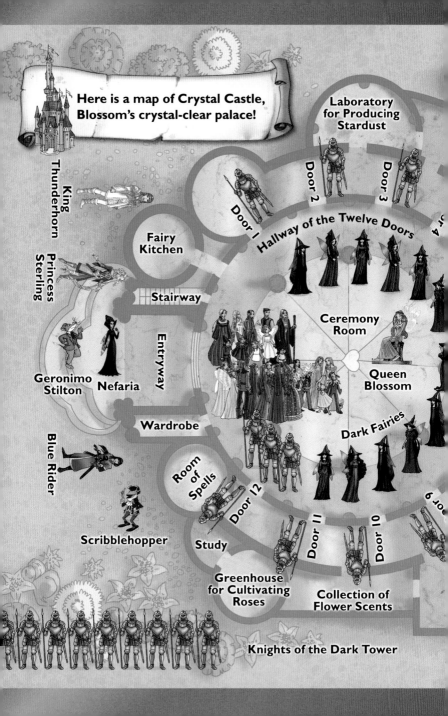

Dragon of the
Rainbow

Fairy Library

White Rose
Labyrinth

Door 5

Parlor for the Flower Fairies

Door 6

Path

Open Door

Castle Garden

Door 7

Fairy
Music

Stairway

Door 8

Crystal Castle is very
big. On the first floor
is the Ceremony
Room and Blossom's
throne. Around
this room, there is a
hallway with twelve
doors. Outside,
there is a garden
and the White Rose
Labyrinth.

Blossom's
Study

Fairy
Advisors'
Study

Chatterclaws

Sparkle

There were giants (who could only put their heads through the windows because they were too **TALL** to enter!), flower fairies, water nymphs, **UNICORNS**, gnomes, and even strange creatures who appeared to be half **rooster** and half **snake**!

I followed a path of rose petals until I saw the queen.

Nice to see you again, dear queen!

Queen Blossom sat on her CRYSTAL throne waiting for me. How strange! Usually, Blossom comes to meet me with OPEN ARMS. Even stranger, she didn't say one word. She just stared at me in silence.

Had she twisted an ankle? Lost her voice? Woken up on the wrong side of her crystal bed?

No Guide! No Armor! No Map!

inally, the queen looked at me with a **STRANGE** expression and announced in a strange voice, "Knight, I order you to listen to me without interrupting!"

How **strange**. Blossom had never given me orders in the past!

Misery   WICKIDA   GRIMELDA   Bitter

I noticed that she was surrounded by a group of fairies with **purple** hair and **POINTY** hats. Several of them held black roses in their hands. They were Dark Fairies, the queen's strange new court!

I was dying to ask the queen what was going on with her new and, um, **SCARY-LOOKING** fairy court, but just then she shouted, "People of the Kingdom of Fantasy! Hear ye, hear ye! I, Queen Blossom,

RESENTIA   HATEFUL   EVILLA

order the knight to go in search of the Sweet Dreams Cradle, which is kept in Munchy Valley by the Munchy Wizards!"

A gasp erupted from the crowd.

"Not MUNCHY VALLEY!"

"Those wizards are pure evil!"

"He'll never make it back alive!"

"We better start carving his tombstone, and

The Sweet Dreams Cradle

find a nice spot in HERO CEMETERY!"

I turned as WHITE as a ball of mozzarella. Oh, how do I get myself into these scary situations!

"Well, Knight. Do you refuse to obey?" Blossom demanded.

Her words ECHOED through the enormouse room.

Sir Geronimo of Stilton

Disappeared during a hopeless mission to Munchy Valley. Burned at the stroke of a magic wand.

Do you refuse to obey?
Do you refuse to obey?
Do you refuse to obey?
Do you refuse to obey?
Do you refuse to obey?
Do you refuse to obey?
Do you refuse to obey?
Do you refuse to obey?
Do you refuse to obey?
Do you refuse to obey?
Do you refuse to obey?
Do you refuse to obey?
Do you refuse to obey?
Do you refuse to obey?
Do you refuse to obey?
Do you refuse to obey?
Do you refuse to obey?
Do you refuse to obey?
Do you refuse to obey?
Do you refuse to obey?
Do you refuse to obey?
Do you refuse to obey?
Do you refuse to obey?
Do you refuse to obey?
Do you refuse to obey?
Do you refuse to obey?
Do you refuse to obey?
Do you refuse to obey?
Do you refuse to obey?
Do you refuse to obey?
Do you refuse to obey?

What could I do? Everyone was waiting for me. "Um, well, I guess, if you really want me to . . . that is, I mean . . . I can try," I mumbled. After all, I didn't want to disappoint Blossom. She had always been so kind to me.

Then I remembered something. "By the way," I asked. "Who will be my guide on this **dangerous** mission?"

Blossom snorted. "You'll have no guide!" she said.

No guide?

I was shocked. "But will I at least have ARMOR to be able to defend myself?" I squeaked.

"No armor!" the queen answered.

No armor?!

Worried, I pleaded, "Can I at least have a map to find the **VALLEY OF THE MUNCHY WIZARDS**?"

At this, Blossom just **ROLLED** her eyes. I took that to mean "no map."

No map?!?

What a nightmare! I excused myself, trying not to burst out in uncontrollable sobs.

Sigh!

Blossom left, followed by the DARK FAIRIES. It was an odd sight — the queen's eyes seemed as **cold** as the strange dark fairies'. And I could hear the crowd murmuring.

"Poor knight."

"The queen was so mean to him."

The queen was so harsh!

Hmm . . .   How strange!   Poor knight!

Yep, my dear friend Blossom had definitely changed since the last time I saw her!

But I had to believe she was still the same person deep inside. And I couldn't **disappoint** her.

Did you hear?

The queen was so rude!

Who knows why · · ·

RIIIBBBIIIITTTT!

ven though I didn't have a guide, armor, or a map, I had an idea. I would ask my friends from my previous trips to the Kingdom of Fantasy to help me!

First, I looked for **Chatterclaws**, who was at the port **swimming** with his family. He waved excitedly. "I'm so whatchamacallit — happy to see you!" he cried.

Sir Geronimo of Stilton's Friends

Chatterclaws the hermit crab helped Geronimo on his seventh adventure; he met the gnome Factual on the first voyage; the chameleon Boils helped on Geronimo's second trip; and First Volume Encyclopedicus (Vol) and Honor the Talking Pen accompanied him on his fifth adventure.

Then he whispered, "I hate to tell you, but whoseywhatsy, I mean the queen, has **FORBIDDEN** me to come with you. But I want to give you this thingamajig. I think it will be **useful** to you."

He rummaged in his shell and offered me a . . . **COMPASS**!

compass

After I left Chatterclaws, I found some of my other old friends. I hoped they might be able to accompany me, but they were all also FORBIDDEN. Still, each one gave me something special.

Boils gave me some **CANDY**, Factual gave me **BERRY JUICE**, Vol gave me a supply of **scrolls**, and Honor gave me a bottle of **ink**.

Boils, could you . . .

1

No can do, Your Knightliness. The queen said I can't come!

Factual, maybe you . . .

2

Knight, I am so, so sorry, but the queen will not allow it!

Lastly, I decided to ask Scribblehopper, my frog friend from my first trip to the kingdom. His house looked like a *water lily* and floated in the center of a pond. When I hit the doorbell, it croaked out,

"RIIIIIIBBBBBIIIIIIITTTTTTTTT!"

Vol, do you think . . .

3

Sorry, Blossom spelled it out in black and white: N-O!

Honor, couldn't you . . .

4

The queen isn't letting me come. It's the truth!

The door opened, and Scribblehopper peeked out.

"Hi, **old friend**! How are you? I was wondering —" I began.

Right then he reached out and **grabbed** me by the tie. Huh? I knew the frog liked fashion, but did he have to steal my favorite tie? Before I

Scribblehopper's House
3 Water Lily Way
Sludge District
Enchanted City
Kingdom of Fantasy

Scribblehopper's Bed

could protest, he YANKED me inside.

"I can help you, but we must be careful. There are SPIES everywhere!" Scribblehopper croaked. Then he gave me a warm hug.

I looked around the frog's house. It had a view of the Croaky Marsh, and a bed shaped like a lily pad. On the walls were pictures of Scribblehopper's ancestors. There was even a picture of Grandma Warty!

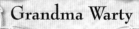

Grandma Warty

"First and foremost, we must have a SNACK!" Scribblehopper insisted, **bustling** around his kitchen. A minute later, he had whipped up a fly-and-gnat sandwich and sludge-filled smoothies.

"Try this, Knight," he said.

I shook my head, trying not to gag.

"Suit yourself," the frog croaked, chomping away.

YUCK!

"Um, I'm actually here to ask if you can help me find the Sweet Dreams Cradle," I explained.

Scribblehopper croaked, "The queen has forbidden me to come with you, Sir Geronimo,

but I have something that will help you."

He pulled out an enormouse **book**. "Do you remember when I told you I wanted to write a book? Well, I finally wrote it! It's a complete **GUIDE** to the Kingdom of Fantasy!

"I titled it . . .

THE LEGENDARIUM!"

BLUE BOG
BODY WASH

FROG LIBRARY

SWAMP WATER
SPRING BATH

LILY PAD BED

SLUDGY SWAMP
SMOOTHIE

MEET SCARLETHOPPER!

have another surprise," Scribblehopper continued. He **knocked** on a little door. "Sweetheart, the knight is here!" he called.

Scribblehopper and his daughter,
Scarlethopper

The door opened, and a young and **fascinating frog** with green skin and flaming red hair came out. She was wearing a fancy **red gown** with lots of lace and a **gold crown** on her head.

She smiled at me and croaked, "Do you recognize me, Knight?"

I stared at her, confused. Something about the frog seemed **familiar**, but I just couldn't place my paw on it.

She held up a scarlet feather and winked.

I gasped. It was a feather from the . . .

Phoenix of Destiny!

Phoenix Feather

Then Scarlethopper **twirled** in a circle and sang, *"Red feather, upon my word, turn me into a flaming bird!"*

Red feather, upon my word, turn me into a flaming bird!

Scarlethopper's Secret

Scarlethopper, Scribblehopper's daughter, is a frog . . . but she can transform into a phoenix! She met Sir Geronimo of Stilton on his first trip to the Kingdom of Fantasy, when he helped her flee from Cackle, the queen of the witches.

Phoenixes are mysterious birds, with fiery red feathers. They are symbols of immortality because they never die. Every five hundred years they are reborn and begin a new life!

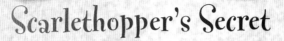

Phoenix feathers are fiery red!

Phoenixes eat incense and perfumed herbs!

Phoenixes sing with a melodious voice!

The Legendarium was written with a magical feather!

Mysterious places are mapped out in The Legendarium!

The Legendarium was made with special paper!

Ah, yes, it was all coming back to me. On my first journey to the Kingdom of Fantasy, Scribblehopper had told me a **SECRET**. His daughter had been transformed into a red phoenix.

"Meet Scarlethopper, Knight. She's my **darling** daughter!" explained Scribblehopper. "We managed to break part of the **spell** that turned her into a phoenix, so now she can also be a **FROG** sometimes! For years, Scarlet has been flying all over the Kingdom of Fantasy and reporting back to me. Thanks to her, I was able to write about all the mysterious places in the kingdom in my *Legendarium*. I wrote the book with one of Scarlet's **magical** feathers on paper made from rare **FLOWER PETALS**."

Scribblehopper held up the **heavy** book proudly. "This is it, Knight. This is my precious *Legendarium*. I'm telling you, it may just save your life. But please don't lose it. It's my **ONLY COPY**!"

Cheese niblets! The Legendarium is . . . legendary!

THE MAKING OF *THE LEGENDARIUM!*

For years, I dreamed of writing a book, and I finally wrote it! I worked day and night, gathering information and maps of unknown places for those who want to travel in the Kingdom of Fantasy.

My daughter described the mysterious places she visited as she flew to every corner of the land!

I used rare flower petals to make the paper for my book.

Finally, I am a real author!

I used a magical red phoenix feather to write every word.

THE NOT-SO-GREAT NEIGHBORHOOD

I THANKED Scribblehopper for *The Legendarium*. The information in it was great! The only thing that was not so great: That book weighed a **TON**! I practically broke my tail lifting it!

Besides the book, the frog insisted I'd need some other supplies. "We will **find** them in a shop that belongs to the cousin of the uncle of the wife of the son of the girlfriend of the barber of my aunt Croaky's plumber. It's called Scarfur's Stealthy Stuff, and it's in the **NOT-SO-GREAT NEIGHBORHOOD** at the edge of Enchanted City," he explained.

We left in the cold night air . . .

As we walked, I looked around. Squeak, what

a **nasty** place! My whiskers trembled with fright.

THERE WERE MEAN-EYED WOLVES

sniffing me hungrily . . .

THERE WERE FOXES WITH SCRUFFY FUR

glaring at me suspiciously . . .

THERE WERE OWLS WHO HOOTED GLOOMILY,

giving me the chills . . .

THERE WERE CREEPY GNOMES

carrying mushrooms that looked deadly . . .

THERE WERE FAIRIES WHO LOOKED LIKE WITCHES

ducking down dark alleys . . .

THERE WERE BUG-EYED BATS

making faces at everyone passing by . . .

There were hidden werewolves

howling fiercely . . .

THERE WERE GHOST KNIGHTS

challenging each other to deadly duels . . .

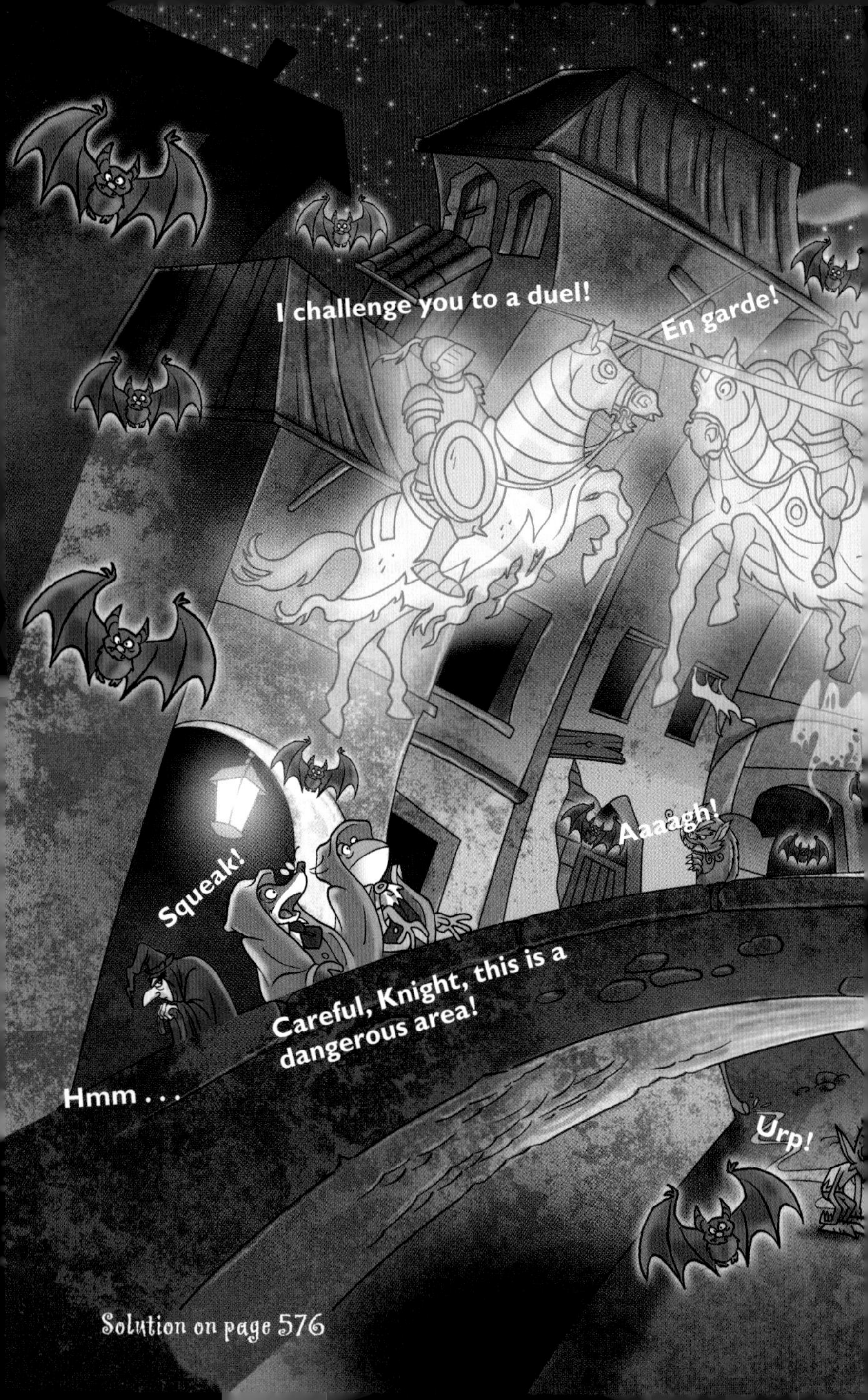

Solution on page 576

How many bats are hiding in this neighborhood?
Screech!
Grrr!
Humpf!
Roar!
Ha, ha, ha!
Hoo! Hoo!
Hum dee hum!

After about **TEN TRILLION FIVE HUNDRED AND SEVENTY-NINE YEARS** (or, okay, maybe just an hour or two), we arrived at a spooky shop with bars on the windows.

The sign read:

SCARFUR'S STEALTHY STUFF

Scribblehopper pushed me forward, and with my heart **pounding**, I went through the door . . .

pounding pounding
pounding
pounding pounding
pounding pounding
pounding pounding pounding
pounding pounding
pounding

WHAT DO YOU EXPECT?

The inside of the store was DIMLY LIT. It was packed with tons of almost-old stuff, kind-of-old stuff, and really old stuff.

I saw scrolls that had grown YELLOW over time, BOATS in bottles, chipped plates, frameless paintings, **flea-ridden** clothes, and lots of other junk.

A thin rodent with dark fur approached us. He had a **SCAR** on his right cheek and a **black patch** over one eye. He wore a sailor's coat and a stained puffy shirt . . .

He was **Scarfur**!

"Welcome to my store, Mister . . . Mister . . . what is your name?" said the rat.

Scribblehopper **hopped** forward, placing a bag of coins on the counter. "Scar, we are here on a private matter. No names, understand?" he croaked.

Scarfur

They say that at one time Scarfur the rat was a pirate in command of a ghost ship! He is the owner of the store Scarfur's Stealthy Stuff in the Not-So-Great Neighborhood, where he sells everything you can't find in any other store in the Kingdom of Fantasy.

SECRET ROOM

Solution on page 576

Scarfur quickly snatched the COINS. "Certainly!" he agreed. "What can I do for you?"

"First, we need some armor for the mouse," Scribblehopper began.

Scarfur brought us to the Secret Room and showed us some golden armor. It looked valuable at a glance, but it was just tin that had been spray-painted gold!

When we grumbled in disappointment, Scar snorted. "What do you expect at that price?"

Scribblehopper sighed. "Well, okay, but I also need a BODYGUARD to accompany the mouse all the way to Munchy Valley."

Scarfur's eyes opened *wide*. Well, at

least his one eye flew open. I couldn't tell about the other one, since he was wearing that patch. "Aha! Now I understand why you are being so *mysterious*, froggy. I'm guessing your friend here might just be the knight who the queen called to —" He stopped midsentence when Scribblehopper shot him a **LOOK**. "Gotcha, greeny. Mum's the word. And don't worry, I've got just the bodyguard for you."

With that, he turned toward the back of the shop and shrieked, "Teeny Sugarsnout! Get your tail out here!"

An enormouse rat with a telescope around his neck arrived from the back room. He was chewing what looked like a piece of taffy, and more *candy* spilled out of his pockets. He was so ***big***, he smashed his head against the doorframe. "Argh!" he whined.

"Seriously? You hit your head again?!" Scarfur snorted. Then he turned to us. "Meet my nephew, **TEENY**. He will be the mouse's bodyguard to Munchy Valley."

Teeny blinked. "Huh? **MUNCHY VALLEY?** But, Uncle, that place is **DANGEROUS**," he complained. Then he felt my muscles. "This mouse is PUNY," he added.

"Of course he's puny! That's why he needs a bodyguard!" Scarfur shrieked.

Teeny Sugarsnout
He's big and beefy, and he's not that bright. Teeny is Scarfur's nephew. One thing you should know about Teeny: He loves chewy caramels and taffy!

Clang!

Clang!

Clang!

I put on the armor made of cheap tin. It felt, well, like it was made of cheap tin. Oh, where can you find a good suit of armor these days?

"Don't worry. Teeny will bring you back, **dead or alive**!" Scarfur assured me.

My knees rattled with fright. "I'd prefer alive," I squeaked.

"Of course," the rat replied. "But if you croak, I've got a beautiful oak **COFFIN** you might like . . ."

I tried to squeak a response, but instead I fainted!

FROG TEARS

When I came to, Scarfur was yelling at Scribblehopper. "Frog, don't think we're done here. The money you gave me isn't enough to pay your bill!"

Scribblehopper explained that the gold he had used was his entire life savings.

"Oh, cry me a river!" the rat scoffed. Then he pointed to Scribblehopper's beautiful red jacket with the gold BUTTONS. "If you give me that coat, I'll settle the bill," he proposed.

At first I thought Scribblehopper was going to hop home, but then he removed the jacket. Tears SPRANG to his eyes, and I remembered that he had once told me the jacket had been in his FAMILY for generations.

"It's okay, Knight," he croaked. "Everything will be fine — maybe! — and you will come back alive — or dead! — or maybe with just a **chopped off** tail, or ear, or paw, or . . ."

Just thinking about the SCARY adventure ahead of me made me want to find the nearest

How about that jacket, froggy?

But . . .

dragon and fly on out of there. But before I could move, Scribblehopper wrapped me in a **SLIMY** hug.

What could I do? I thanked him for being a **true friend** and told him I was sorry about his coat.

"It's okay," the frog sniffed, but I could tell the **waterworks** were about to start again. "That jacket was inherited from my great-great-great-grandfather. The red silk came from the islands of the Scarlet Worms, and it was stitched with a golden needle by my ancestor, the tailor Scissorhopper."

Scissorhopper

Then Scribblehopper went off into the **DARK** night, and I was left with Teeny to go off in search of the *Sweet Dreams cradle*.

It was going to be a dangerous trip, and the night was **freezing**. Rats! I was feeling more terrified by the minute. Still, the memory of the sacrifice that my friend had made for me warmed my **HEART**.

TRUE FRIENDSHIP WARMS YOUR HEART!

THE SWEET
DREAMS CRADLE

CHOCK-FULL OF INFO!

I leafed through *The Legendarium* and found a lot of information about all the Mysterious Places in the Kingdom of Fantasy, like . . .

- **MUNCHY VALLEY**, home of the gluttonous Munchy Wizards.
- **Batlandia**, the land of the stinkiest bats.
- **FANG COUNTY**, where the vicious Vile Vampires live.
- **HAIRY WOODS**, the forest that houses the Three Green Hairballs.
- **WAVE CASTLE**, the underwater home of the mysterious wizard Lakeness.
- **MOUNT GIANT**, the peninsula where Redhot the Giant Dragon lives.
- **Melancholy Village**, where everyone becomes really sad.

Scribblehopper was right. That book was **chock-full** of info!

I found a giant map of the Kingdom of Fantasy, and finally located **MUNCHY VALLEY**, my destination.

This book is priceless!

MAP OF THE KINGDOM OF FANTASY

MYSTERIOUS ABYSS

SEA OF DREAMS

CASTLE OF DREAMS

KINGDOM OF THE PIXIES

LAND OF NIGHTMARES

KINGDOM OF THE FIRE DRAGONS

KINGDOM OF THE FAIRIES

KINGDOM OF THE MERMAIDS

LAND OF TROLLS

CITY OF THE BLUE UNICORNS

KINGDOM OF THE WITCHES

KINGDOM OF THE DIGGERTS

LAND OF TOYS

LAND OF SWEETS

LAND OF THE OGRES

The map can change at any moment, because the places in the Kingdom of Fantasy are infinite. In this map, the Mysterious Places are also shown: places that no one has seen until now!

SEA OF DREAMS

KINGDOM OF THE SEA

KINGDOM OF THE GNOMES

DESERT OF EYES AND EARS

RAINBOW VALLEY

TALKING FOREST

REALM OF THE TOWERING PEAKS

KINGDOM OF THE NORTHERN GIANTS

KINGDOM OF THE ELVES

KINGDOM OF THE SILVER DRAGONS

LAND OF TIME

KINGDOM OF THE SOUTHERN GIANTS

THE MYSTERIOUS PLACES

1. Munchy Valley
2. Batlandia
3. Fang County
4. Hairy Woods
5. Wave Castle
6. Mount Giant
7. Melancholy Village

WAAA! I TWISTED MY ANKLE!

started walking, but it wasn't easy. Every time I took a **pawstep**, my cheap armor creaked, **clanged**, and rattled. It felt like my whole body was in prison!

Things went from bad to worse when I tripped and **bashed** into Teeny. He fell to the ground

1 Aaaah!

2 Bash! Huh?!

I tripped . . .

. . . and fell on top of Teeny!

crying, "Waaa! I **twisted** my ankle! I can't walk!"

For a big rat, Teeny sure was a crybaby. But I was stuck with him now, and I couldn't give up already. Thinking fast, I built a **WHEELBARROW** out of some branches, and Teeny climbed in.

I pushed him forward, **huffing** and **PUFFING**.

It turned out that Munchy Valley was full of **TRAPS** . . .

3 Waaa!

He began to yell . . .

Huff . . . puff!

It's all your fault!

4

. . . and in the end I had to push him!

TRAPDOOR

OPPOSITES CROSSROAD

FALSE FOUNTAIN

STOMACHACHE TREE

1 We fell into a trapdoor — well, it was really a hole covered by a bunch of leaves.

2 We arrived at OPPOSITES CROSSROAD, with paths pointing RIGHT and LEFT — even though they both ended at the same point.

3 We stopped at the False Fountain, which advertised "Water that tastes better than chocolate!" We drank it, and it tasted like rancid squeeze cheese.

4 We found a STOMACHACHE TREE and tasted its fruit, and we got — you guessed it — stomachaches!

5 We found a bottle of

perfume labeled "**THE SWEETEST SCENT EVER**," but when we tried it, we stunk like sour milk.

(6) We crossed the **Itchy Woods** and began scratching like flea-bitten sewer rats.

(7) We passed by a lever marked "**SURPRISE!**" I tried to stop Teeny (I had had enough surprises to last a lifetime!), but he pulled the lever anyway. We were hit with an avalanche of rocks.

Finally, at dusk, I saw a castle that was made entirely of **COOKIES**. This was it: Munchy Castle, of the Munchy Wizards!

THE SWEETEST
SCENT EVER

ITCHY
WOODS

SURPRISE
LEVER

MUNCHY VALLEY

1. Trapdoor
2. Opposites Crossroad
3. False Fountain
4. Stomachache Tree
5. Bottle of the Sweetest Scent Ever
6. Itchy Woods
7. Surprise Lever
8. Alchemy Avenue: leads to Munchy Castle
9. Munchy Castle
10. Magnetic Mountain: attracts metal

COOKIE

Cookie is the queen of the Munchy Wizards. She is obsessed with baking and eating cookies and won't let any of her cooks use their own recipes. Her motto is "Cook it my way or hit the highway!"

Cookie is always cranky, because she suffers from insomnia. The only way she can fall asleep is to listen to the melodies of the Sweet Dreams Cradle.

Cook it my way or hit the highway!

Cookie's magic wand has a spoon on one end and a fork on the other.

THE MUNCHY WIZARDS

Instead of flying on brooms like many wizards do, the Munchy Wizards fly on giant forks.

Griller

Cookette

Snips

Stitchita

Dishy

Accountina

Greenie

A Castle Made of Cookies!

Munchy Castle looked good enough to eat. Who can resist a **tasty** cookie? Still, I knew better than to take even one nibble. There were **threatening** signs posted everywhere.

KEEP OUT!

GET LOST OR GET BURNED!

NO TRESPASSING!

ONLY COOKS ALLOWED!

SHOO! SCRAM!

I was hoping Teeny would stick around, but right then he announced, "Well, I'm **out of here**. I delivered you to the castle, and my job is done."

COOK IT MY WAY OR HIT THE HIGHWAY

Rats! **Trembling** with fear, I **CLINK**-clank-**CLUNKED** over to a bush near the front door.

How would I get inside?

Right at that moment, the door burst open . . .

Griller, one of the Munchy Wizards, was shoving another wizard dressed like a cook out the door. "Where'd you learn how to cook? **Puke Pastry University?!**" Griller shrieked. "Those cookies you made almost killed the queen! Didn't you notice the edges weren't golden brown the way she likes them?"

The cook rolled her eyes. "Golden brown, **CRUNCHY**, chewy, five chips on this one, ten walnuts on that one . . . How can anyone remember all those ridiculous rules? Forget **cookie the Wizard**. That queen is just plain cuckoo!" she fumed.

As I watched, the cook **ripped** off her apron and hat, threw them on the ground, and stormed off.

That queen is cuckoo!

Get out!

SHOO!

SCRAM!

KEEP OUT!

GET LOST!

Where are the cook's spoon, fork, and rolling pin hidden?

Solution on page 576

Straw

Hat and apron

Muddy stick and blackberries

As soon as the door closed, I came up with an ***idea***. I would dress myself up like a cook and **sneak** into the castle. I picked up the hat and apron that the cook had left on the ground, and I stuffed my clothes with **LEAVES** so I would be as big as the Munchy Wizards.

Finally, I used straw to weave a wig and a muddy stick to make eyelashes, and I stained my lips with **bLackbeRRieS** to look like lipstick.

NOW I REALLY LOOKED LIKE A MUNCHY WIZARD!

CAREFUL,
OR I'LL BURN YOU!

I gathered my courage and knocked on the door. Knock! **Knock! Knock!**

"Go away! I'm not interested!" a voice yelled from inside.

"Ahem, it is I, Geronimosa. I'm here to apply for the cooking job," I squeaked in my best lady voice.

The door burst open, and Griller shrieked, "That was **FAST**! I never even advertised! Well, don't just stand there — come in. I'm taking you straight to Cookie. Just don't say anything stupid. She's in a **terrible** mood!"

I tried to smile, but I was so nervous, I chewed my whiskers instead.

Griller led me down a **DARK** hallway right

to the wizard queen, **COOKIE**!

She was dressed all in black and was carrying a strange object that was half fork and half spoon. I recognized it from *The Legendarium*. It was **the Wandinator**, the magic wand she used to **BURN** anyone who annoyed her!

GREASY blond hair poked out of Cookie's

Cookie, your wish is my command!

It better be, or I'll burn you!

The Wandinator,
Cookie's magic wand

pointed black hat, and her dress was streaked with chocolate. Her teeth were full of **cavities**. Something told me Cookie's last trip to the dentist had been sometime between never and never.

"Hello. I'm Geronimosa," I began.

But Cookie held up her hand. "Enough with the chit-chat, cook! Can't you see I'm **starving** here?! Go to the kitchen and make me a batch of cookies. And they better be good, or I'll burn you with the Wandinator!" she demanded.

Bzzzt!

"Your wish is my command," I told Cookie. I bowed my head low — and

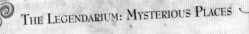

THE SWEET DREAMS CRADLE

The Sweet Dreams Cradle is made of gold
and decorated with a giant pearl, a blue
sapphire, and a green emerald.

It produces a song that makes everyone
sleep soundly. It is said that the cradle is
the work of the famous gemologist Marvin
McDreamy, who specialized in enchanted
jewelry. McDreamy made it for himself
because he suffered from insomnia. The
wizard queen Cookie stole it to help her
own insomnia.

*To make the cradle play,
pull the red ribbon tied to
the emerald . . . you will
hear a sweet melody that
will make you sleep!*

that's when I spotted it. Cookie was wearing a bejeweled **GOLD** pendant around her neck. It was the treasure I was looking for, the **Sweet Dreams Cradle**! I had read about in *The Legendarium*!

Cookie left, and I went in search of the kitchen. But the castle was so enormouse, I got lost in a **maze** of hallways all made out of cookies!

I turned and turned in that cookie labyrinth until finally I reached the Munchy Castle's kitchen . . .

HELP GERONIMO MAKE IT THROUGH THE LABYRINTH!

ENTER

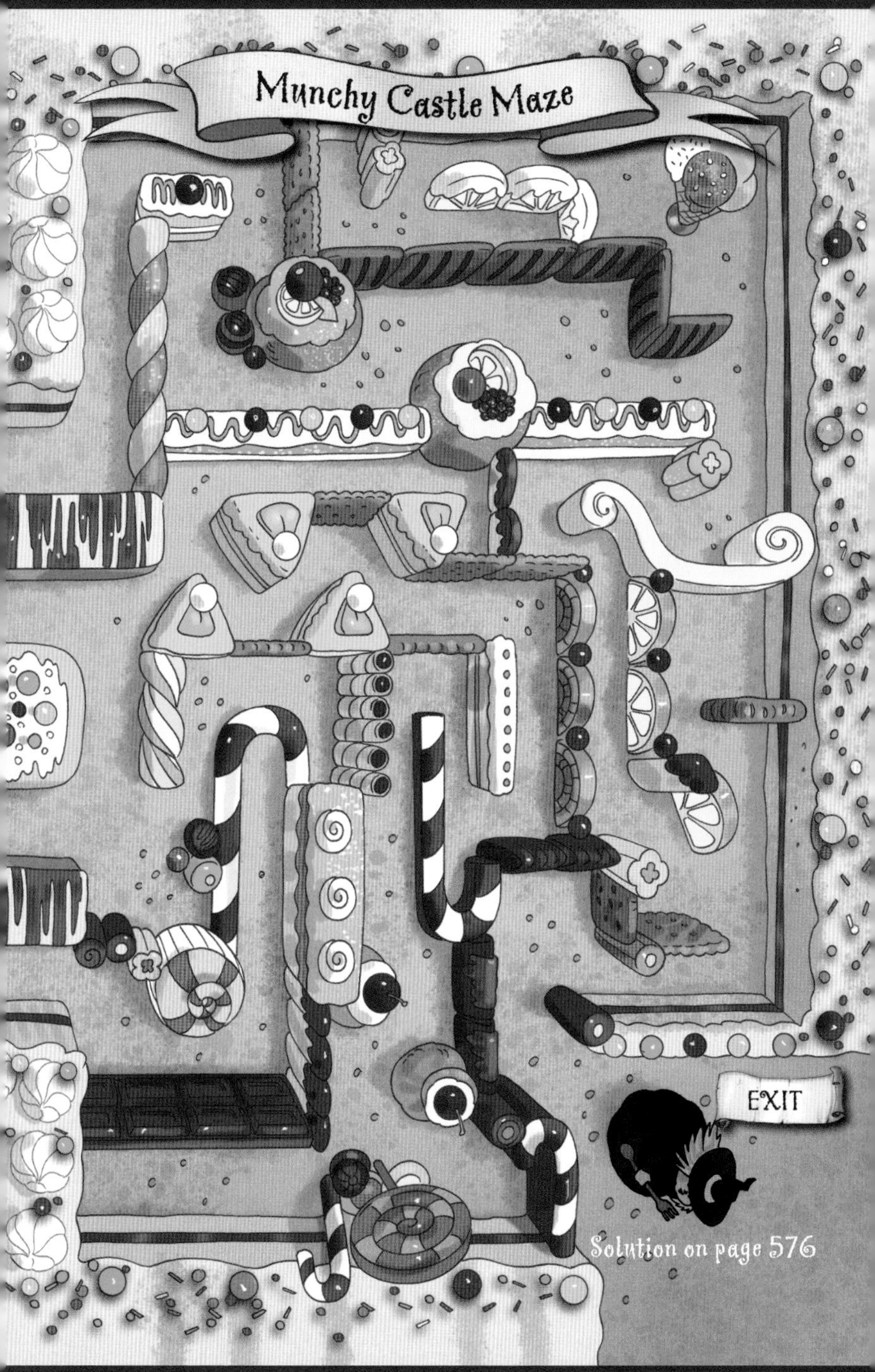

Munchy Castle Maze

EXIT

Solution on page 576

DARK CHOCOLATE OR MILK CHOCOLATE?

I n the kitchen, I started **scampering** around like that super-energetic cooking show host Rachael Rat. I racked my brains trying to remember the recipe I had been trying at home for **extra-chewy, extra-chocolaty chocolate chip cookies**. Had I used dark chocolate or milk chocolate? One cup of sugar or two?

I **EXPERIMENTED** all day, and in the evening, I took the cookies out of the oven . . .

Will she like my cookies? Eek, I hope so!

1 I didn't remember the cookie recipe, so I tried and tried and tried new things all day . . .

2 In the evening, I finally took the perfect chocolate chip cookies out of the oven!

EXTRA-CHEWY, EXTRA-CHOCOLATY
CHOCOLATE CHIP COOKIES

Ask an adult to help you!

INGREDIENTS

½ cup softened butter
⅓ cup brown sugar
⅓ cup granulated sugar
1 egg

½ tsp vanilla
1-¼ cup flour
½ tsp salt
½ tsp baking soda
1 cup chocolate chips

1. Beat together the butter and sugar. Add egg and vanilla. In a separate bowl, combine flour, salt, and baking soda. Stir flour mixture into egg mixture. Add chocolate chips.

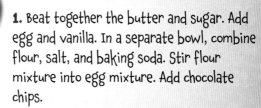

2. Make a log out of the dough and wrap it in parchment paper. Leave in the fridge for at least two hours.

3. Preheat the oven to 375° F. Cut the log into half-inch slices and put them on an ungreased baking sheet. Leave a little space between the cookies.

4. Cook them at 375°F for 8–10 minutes.

WHO STOLE MY CRADLE?

ookie sniffed the cookies and muttered, "**Hmm . . .**"

Then she put a cookie in her mouth and muttered, "**Umm . . .**" Then she swallowed the cookie and muttered, "**Hmm . . .**"

What did it mean? Just when I thought I would

Here are the cookies!

Chomp . . . burp!

faint from fear, Cookie's face lit up, and she cried, "Delicious!"

She ate a few more cookies (well, eight to be exact, but who's counting).

"Not bad, Geronimosa. Here's your reward," she said, handing me a **GOLDEN** box. "These are Munchy Sweets. They're so yummy, we wizards use them as money," she said. Then she went off to bed.

Munchy Sweets

Munchy Sweets are caramels made using 333 different ingredients, including vanilla, mint, licorice, cherries, honey, ginger, rhubarb, and many more!

I waited until all the Munchy Wizards went to sleep, then I climbed up a **THORNY** vine leading to Cookie's bedroom window. Cookie was climbing under the covers. A minute later, she tugged the eMeRALD on the cradle, and it began playing soothing music.

Cookie yawned and placed the cradle on her nightstand. Then she began to snore . . .

"Zzzzzzzzzzzzzzz!
Zzzzzzzzzzzzzzz!
Zzzzzzzzzzzzzzz!
Zzzzzzzzzzzzzzz!"

This was it! The perfect time to get my paws on the cradle!

I yanked the chef's hat over my ears so I wouldn't hear the MUSIC and fall asleep. Then I opened the window and SCAMPERED over to Cookie's nightstand. I grabbed the cradle. Success!

Clutching the cradle, I headed toward the window on my TIPPY-PAWS. But right at that moment, I tripped on the carpet and fell snoutfirst on the floor. Rancid rat hairs! It woke Cookie up, and she started yelling. "Hey! Who stole my cradle? When I catch who did it, I'll burn her to a crisp!"

MARZIPAN CEILING

SPONGE CAKE WALLS

CHOCOLATE AND COOKIE BED

CARAMELIZED NIGHTSTAND

STRAWBERRY-FLAVORED CARPET

Then she began to throw everything she could find at me, even her heavy CHAMBER POT. I was climbing

COOKIE THE WIZARD'S CHAMBER POT

down the vine as fast as I could, until disaster struck. Cookie took a giant pair of SCISSORS and cut the vine. I fell!
fell!
fell!
fell!
fell!
fell!
fell!
fell!
fell!
fell!
fell!

I DON'T WANT
TO BE BURNED!

As soon as I hit the ground, I **ran** to the bushes, where I found Teeny hiding. I was thrilled! I guess the big lug hadn't left me after all. I put my **armor** back on, and we took off at full speed.

The Munchy Wizards raced after us on their **FLYING FORKS**, shooting *LIGHTNING* down from their wands.

Bzzzt! Bzzzzt!

Bzzzt! Bzzzzt!

Bzzzt! Bzzzzt!

Bzzzt! Bzzzzt!

Bzzzzzzzzzzzzt!

Come back!

Bzzzt! Bzzzt! Bzzzt!

Bzzzt! *Bzzzt!*

Bzzzt!

Bzzzt!

Hope you like fried whiskers!

Bzzzt!

Take that!

Bzzzt!

You're toast!

Bzzzt!

Suddenly, I got an idea. Magnetic Mountain was nearby. It was an enormouse **MAGNET**, so it would attract metal.

We headed in that direction, and all the wizards followed us. Then their **FLYING FORKS** were pulled toward the mountain!

Help!

Come on!

clannnnnng!

Sorry, Knight.

It's okay . . .

"The rat **TRICKED** us!" whined the wizards. While they were still dazed, Teeny and I hightailed it all the way back to Enchanted City. Once there, I realized something **STRANGE**. Teeny's ankle was better! When I mentioned it, the big rat blushed.

"Sorry, Knight. I wasn't really hurt, just tired. And that **WHEELBARROW** you made was so **comfy**," he confessed.

I guess the wizards weren't the only ones who were **TRICKED**! Still, as my aunt Sweetfur says, true friends should be forgiven. So I smiled at

Teeny and gave him the box of **MUNCHY SWEETS**.

chomp chomp chomp chomp chomp chomp chomp chomp chomp chomp chomp chomp chomp chomp chomp chomp chomp chomp chomp chomp

"Thanks!" Teeny exclaimed. "And here is a present for you, Knight." He handed me his telescope.

Waving good-bye to my friend, I headed toward Crystal Castle, whistling happily.

whistling happily whistling happily whistling happily whistling happily whistling happily

LEAVE AT ONCE!

I was feeling **proud**. My mission was accomplished! But when I reached Blossom, a dark fairy ripped the cradle out of my paw. And the leader of the **KNIGHTS OF THE DARK TOWER** glared down at me.

What are you looking at?

Give it here, rat!

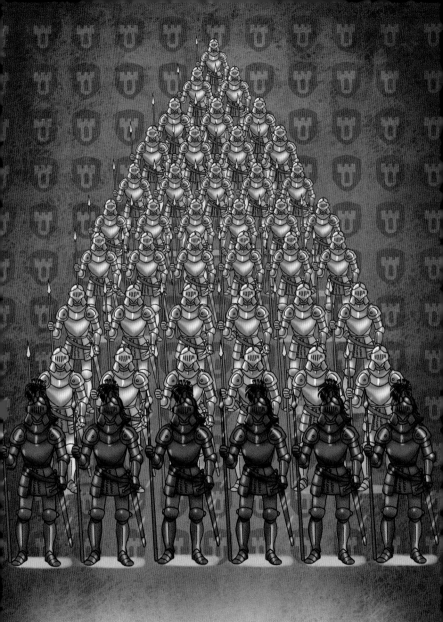

THE KNIGHTS OF THE DARK TOWER

Led by Bighead (the knight with the big head)

Instead of thanking me, Blossom said, "Knight, you must leave again at once! This time, bring me the **ESSENCE OF DARKNESS**, held in Batlandia by the **Tribe of Stinky Bats**!"

I was stunned. "But I just — I mean, that is — I thought . . . " I babbled.

"**LEAVE AT ONCE!**" the queen ordered, pointing to the door.

Leave at once!

Bighead, the leader of the knights, grabbed me by my **tail** and dragged me away.

All the knights of the Dark Tower laughed at me as I passed them . . .

"Ha, ha, ha! That **fake armor** is ridiculous!"

"His sword is made of tinfoil!"

"He's not a knight — he's a **nightmare**!"

I **SCAMPERED** away from them with my tail between my paws. How humiliating!

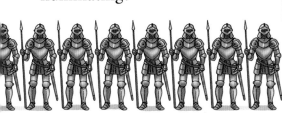

When I left Crystal Castle, it was evening. I sat on a rock, feeling **sad**. But what could I do? I had to get going on my next mission. I studied *The Legendarium*, trying to figure out how to get to Batlandia.

I wondered if I had the strength to make it. I was feeling **so tired** ... so tired ... so tired ... so tired ...

THE ESSENCE OF DARKNESS

WE'RE LISTENING!

Eventually the sun set, and I could no longer read *The Legendarium*. At that moment, I heard a small voice. "What's with the sad face, **GOLDEN** Knight?"

"It's not **gold**; it's just tin that's been painted **gold**. And I'm feeling lonely," I found myself answering.

"You are not alone. I'm listening to you, Knight," replied the voice.

"And I'm **listening**," said another little voice. And then a chorus of voices sang, "We're listening!"

Moldy mozzarella! What was happening? Why was I hearing voices? Had I gone **batty** reading about Batlandia?

I was still trying to figure it out when I saw

them. Fireflies! A whole swarm of twinkling fireflies!

"There is a solution to every problem, Knight. You just need to find it," the **fireflies** told me. Then they sang a little song . . .

Knight . . .

. . . you are not alone . . .

Ooooh!

. . . we are here!

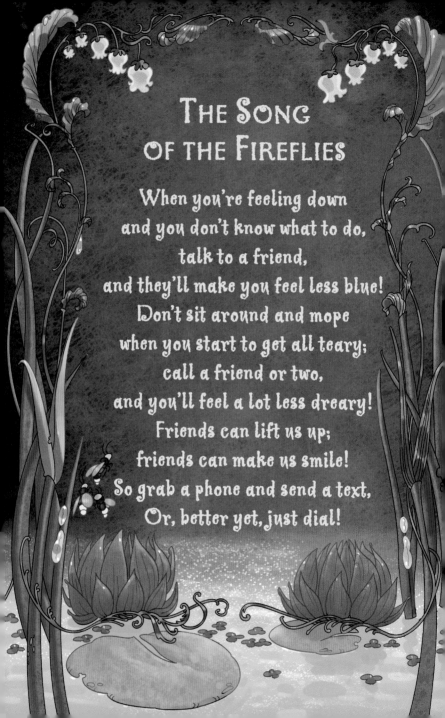

THE SONG OF THE FIREFLIES

When you're feeling down
and you don't know what to do,
talk to a friend,
and they'll make you feel less blue!
Don't sit around and mope
when you start to get all teary;
call a friend or two,
and you'll feel a lot less dreary!
Friends can lift us up;
friends can make us smile!
So grab a phone and send a text,
Or, better yet, just dial!

I have to say, the fireflies' song really **CHEERED** me up. And I was even happier when, after I explained that I was going to Batlandia, one firefly came forward. She wore a SMALL golden crown and spoke in a sweet, calming voice. "I, Queen Twinkle, do hereby declare that we will accompany you on your mission!"

After that, the entire swarm of fireflies got together and formed a soft bed for me to lie on. Then they **CARRIED** me straight to Batlandia!

Twinkle
The Queen of the Fireflies

THAT'S USING YOUR BLINKER!

When I woke up, I wished I hadn't. I had been DREAMING — something about cheesecake, the beach, and a twelve-piece symphony orchestra . . .

Anyway, where was I? Oh, yes. I woke up and found I was in Dreary Batlandia. The fireflies brought me to the **Blackout Maze**, where the Stinky Bats lived.

bat bat bat bat bat bat bat bat bat bat bat bat bat bat bat bat bat bat bat bat bat bat bat bat bat bat bat bat bat bat bat

"I have to find the **ESSENCE OF DARKNESS**," I told Twinkle. "But how will I get it away from the Stinky Bats?"

Flashy, the queen's niece, spoke up. "I've got it!" She blinked. "We offer the bats something they can't resist: **pink stinkbug slushies**! They'll get the slushies in exchange for the Essence of Darkness!"

"Now, that's using your BLINKER!" praised the queen.

The queen divided the fireflies into two teams. One team was to fly north and buy **pink stinkbug syrup**. The other team was

Flashy

The queen's niece. She is a careful observer and full of bright ideas! She is next in line to become queen.

Twinkle and Flashy

sent south to buy ice.

Twinkle opened a chest full of tiny **golden coins**: the treasure of the fireflies.

I felt bad that the fireflies were spending their savings, but the queen waved me off. "What are **friends** for?" she said.

No treasure is worth more than friendship!

1. **Stinky Bats**, who rule Batlandia, live in the Blackout Maze.

2. **Sea Bats** wear green algae.

3. **Pink Bats** announce the arrival of spring.

4. **Purple Bats** have flowing purple hair.

5. **Liar Bats** have shifty eyes.

6. **Lacy Bats** wear fancy shirts.

7. **Ghost Bats** have eerie transparent wings.

8. **Joker Bats** have evil laughs.

9. **Gladiator Bats** carry swords.

10. **Warrior Bats** dress in full armor.

Batty Gorge

Blackout Maze

Batspring Mountain

BATLANDIA

Ghostly Cave

4

5

7

Liar Cave

Purple Basin

6

Fancy Cave

Snarl Cave

8

10

Duel Arena

9

Gladiator Stone
Statue

WHAT'S WORSE THAN A STINKY BAT?

After the fireflies left, I headed into the Blackout Maze. It was a total blackout in there — I couldn't see a thing! Plus, the entrance was so narrow, I had strip down to my underwear to get through!

How embarrassing!

To enter the maze, I had to pass through a bat-shaped hole . . . which I could only fit through by stripping down to my underwear!

The maze **stunk** like a cat's litter box (sorry to gross you out, but it did!), and the whole place was ***swarming*** with stinkbugs!

What a stench!

BLECH!

I kept turning and turning until I reached an enormouse cavern. Over a raging bonfire sat a huge pot of **boiling** liquid.

Thousands of bats flew around. They were pushing the **DARKNESS** of the cavern into the pot by flapping their wings. So this was how they made the **ESSENCE OF DARKNESS**!

As they flew, the bats sang. And do you know what's worse than a stinky bat? A stinky bat who can't carry a **tune**! And I thought *I* was tone deaf!

Ouch!

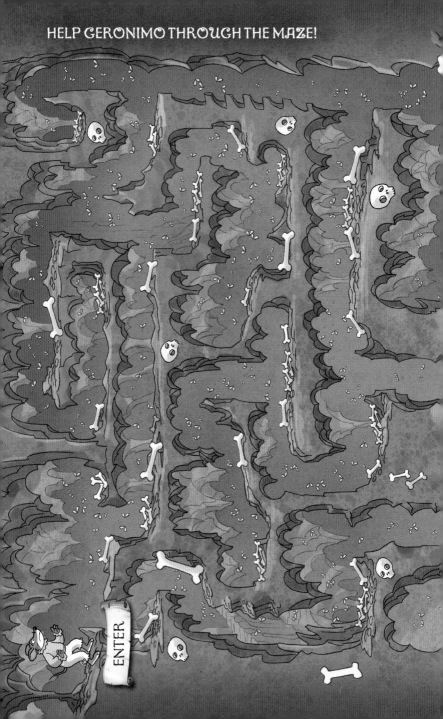

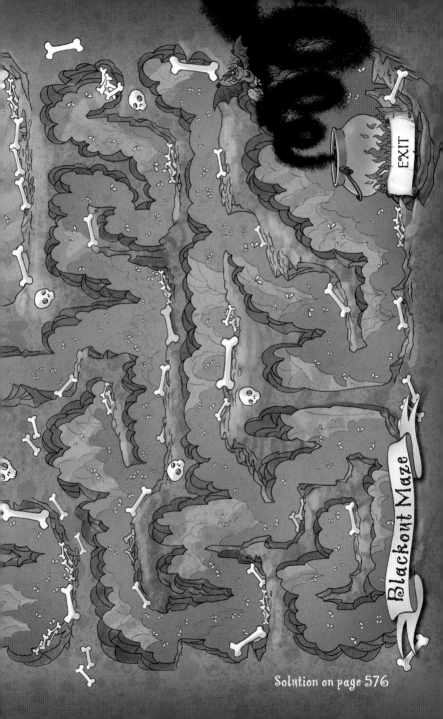

EXIT

Blackout Maze

Solution on page 576

TRIBE OF STINKY BATS

SCREAMY BAT

SNEAKY BAT

ARCHERY BAT

BEEFY BAT

BRAINY BAT

FIXIT BAT

MECHANIC BAT

BUILDY BAT

FLOWER BAT

DOCTOR BAT

BANDAGE BAT AND OUCHY BAT

SNIPPY BAT

KNITSY BAT

SCRIBBLE BAT

MAKEOVER BAT

GRAND POO-BAH BAT: THE STINKIEST BAT!

FOODIE BAT

WOODSY BAT

WORKY BAT

Swarm of stinkbugs

The Stinky Bats' Stinky Cave!

Grand Poo-Bah Bat, the king of the Stinky Bats, sat on a bat throne surrounded by a CLOUD of stinkbugs. Some of the Stinky Bats were THUMPING on drums. Others blew into **screeching** horns. Still others were dancing around and waving clubs.

Between the noise and the smell, I was beginning to feel faint!

WHAT A STENCH!

Who is this mysterious little bat?

I noticed a small bat in the corner. He wasn't singing or dancing, and, even stranger, he didn't stink.

Taking a **DEEP** breath, I stood up and squeaked, "Umm, hello! I am Sir Geronimo of Stilton, and in the name of Queen Blossom, I —"

But before I could finish my sentence, one of the Stinky Bats **BONKED** me over the head with his club!

"Ouch!" I cried. And then I really did FAINT!

Bonk!

Ouch!

FLY SPREAD AND
MOSQUITO SAUCE

hen I came to, I was tied up and two bats were carrying me toward a bat wearing what looked like a CHEF'S HAT. Rats! This wasn't going well.

Foodie Bat, the one with the chef's hat, was carrying a large serving fork. "Yum, mouse

Eep! Eep! Eep! Eep! Eep! Eep! Eep! Eep! Eep! Eep! Eep!

Eep! Eep! Eep! Eep! Eep! Eep!

Eep! Eep! Eep!

Bring him here!

Eep!

Uh-oh!

meat!" he cried. "I tink I vill cook him wiff some **poisonous mushrooms**, cave mold, fly spread, crushed larvae, **termite ragu**, stuffed scorpions, mosquito sauce, gnat mustard, **moth salsa**, bee gelatin, beetle meatballs, insect preserves, and fresh ants! Yes, **ZIS** is vat I vill do!"

I gasped in **HORROR**. Oh, how had it come to **ZIS** — I mean *this*! I had to do something, fast!

"Wait!" I begged. "I have a proposal I think you will like!"

Luckily, the **GRAND POOH-BAH BAT** held up his wings to stop the others. "Okay, vee are listening," he screeched.

Eep! Eep! Eep! Eep! Eep! Eep!

A Pink Stinkbug Slushy

I *QUICKLY* explained to the bats that if they would give me the **ESSENCE OF DARKNESS** I would make them each a delicious, frosty . . .

pink stinkbug slushy!

"Eeep!" the bats cheered. "Vee love zee slushies!"

Right then the **FIREFLIES** arrived, carrying the pink stinkbug syrup and ice. Perfect timing! As the bats watched, I began to whip up the pink slushies, following a secret recipe.

RECIPE FOR
Pink Stinkbug Slushies

IF YOU DON'T HAVE REAL PINK STINKBUG SYRUP, USE FRESH STRAWBERRIES AS A SUBSTITUTE!

Ask an adult to help you!

INGREDIENTS

2 pints of strawberries
3 tsp sugar
½ lemon
10-12 ice cubes

1. Wash the strawberries and cut them into pieces. Put them in a blender with the juice of half a lemon and the sugar.

2. Have an adult blend the ice into the strawberry mixture until the desired consistency is achieved. Serve to your friends and family and enjoy!

 Eep eep eep!

Calm down! There's enough for everyone!

 Eeeep!

I took the ice and mashed it with a rock to **crush** it. Then I poured the pink stinkbug syrup over it and mixed it together.

All the bats got in line and held up their wooden cups for me to fill. Then they slurped up the slushies with little spoons that looked like **(GULP!)** bones!

In exchange for the slushies, the Grand Poo-Bah Bat gave me a box filled with black **DUST**. It was the mysterious **ESSENCE OF DARKNESS**!

It was truly
the essence
of the darkest
darkness!

THE ESSENCE OF DARKNESS

The Essence of Darkness is made up of the dust of crushed bones. This mysterious substance has the power to create darkness so complete an ordinary mouse can't even see his own paw in front of his snout!

Only the Tribe of Stinky Bats knows how to create this dark substance.

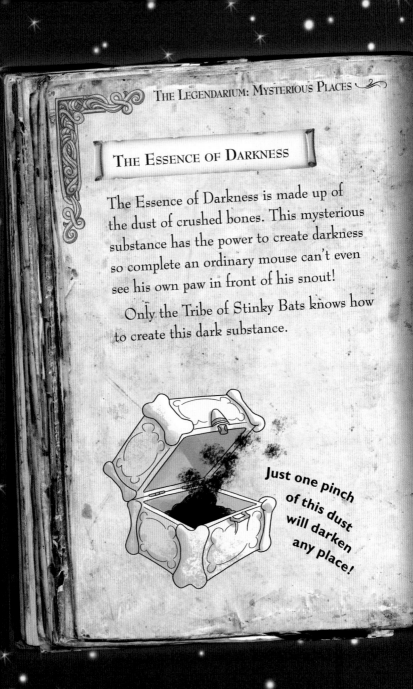

Just one pinch of this dust will darken any place!

Besides the Essence of Darkness, the Stinky Bats also gave me a suit of armor made out of bark. Thank goodmouse! I had left my old armor at the entrance to the Blackout Maze, and after all, I'm a modest mouse. I would have been too humiliated to walk around in just my **UNDERWEAR**!

Once again, I climbed onto the bed of fireflies, and we left.

As we flew, I used the telescope to look at all the many lands beneath me. The Kingdom of Fantasy is such an **ENORMOUSE** place. I guess that's why every time I visit I have a completely new adventure!

Strangely, as I looked around, I had a funny feeling that someone was following me . . .

Finally, we landed at CRYSTAL CASTLE.

Hmmm . . . Is someone following me?

WHATEVER!

s I entered the castle, I still had a **funny** feeling that someone was following me.

Blossom was shocked to see me. "You've returned this time, too? But how did you manage

Here it is . . .

You're here again?!

to escape the Stinky Bats? They are so **DANGEROUS**, and they should have — I mean, they could have **CUT** you to bits!" she snapped.

I tried to explain about the fireflies and the suit of armor and the **pink stinkbug slushies** but she didn't seem interested. "Whatever!" she said, grabbing the box containing the Essence of Darkness.

Then she threw me an **icy** look and ordered, "Since you made it back alive — I mean, for your next mission, you will go to **Fang County**, the home of the Vile Vampires, in search of the CRYSTAL COFFIN.

The Crystal Coffin

Vampires? Coffins? Slimy Swiss cheese, how terrifying!

I tried to get a grip, but I couldn't help myself. I turned as **PALE** as a skeleton . . . as stiff as a mummy . . . and as shaky as a leaf in the wind . . .

But I couldn't say no to Blossom. I nodded and left the castle, and when I got outside I . . .

fainted from the fright!
fainted from the fright!
fainted from the fright!

Ugh . . . I'm a dead mouse!

THE
CRYSTAL COFFIN

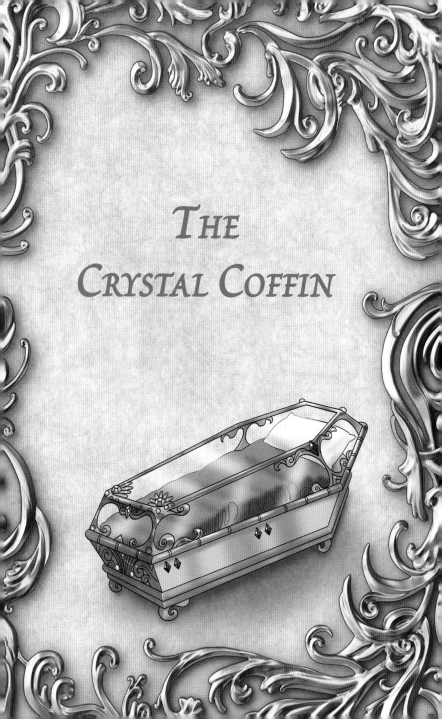

I Can't Stand Stink!

hen I woke up, someone was fanning air at me. I muttered, "Huh? Who are you? Who am I? Why am I dressed in bark?"

In front of me I saw . . . a **BAT**!

The bat smiled kindly and explained who he was.

"DON'T BE AFRAID, KNIGHT! I AM THE SON OF THE KING OF THE STINKY BATS. I WON'T HURT YOU!"

Only then did I **RECOGNIZE** him. It was the Stinky Bat who had been off on his own at the

Stinky Bats' Stinky Cave.

"I followed you here, Knight, because I want to help you on your mission. My name is Spitfire Bat, and this is my story . . .

SPITFIRE'S STORY

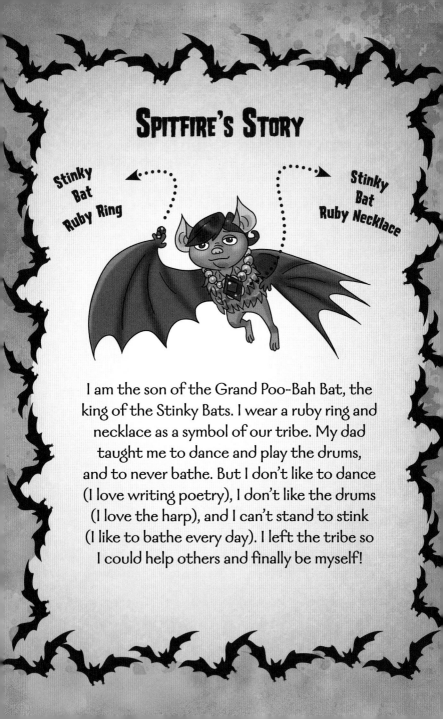

Stinky
Bat
Ruby Ring

Stinky
Bat
Ruby Necklace

I am the son of the Grand Poo-Bah Bat, the
king of the Stinky Bats. I wear a ruby ring and
necklace as a symbol of our tribe. My dad
taught me to dance and play the drums,
and to never bathe. But I don't like to dance
(I love writing poetry), I don't like the drums
(I love the harp), and I can't stand to stink
(I like to bathe every day). I left the tribe so
I could help others and finally be myself!

"So, anyway, Knight. Can I come with you on your **HEROIC MISSION**?" the bat concluded.

I **shook** my head. "I can't bring you along," I told the bat. "I'm going to this very **DANGEROUS** place in **Fang County**, the home of the Vile Vampires."

At the word *vampires*, Spitfire's ears perked up. "But that's perfect! In a county of vampires, you'll need to pretend that you are a **VAMPIRE**, too, and a bat assistant will come in handy!"

I had to admit that he was right. So I agreed. But first Spitfire insisted I needed a good vampire disguise. He led me to a store called The Phony Factory.

THE PHONY FACTORY

The store was full of all sorts of costumes. There were **wigs** and wings and masked **dummies**. Everything looked so real, it was hard to tell what was fake.

An **old woman** with a very long nose jumped out at us.

"Hello, I am Leapy Longnoser! Welcome to the Phony Factory!"

The Phony Factory

This store specializes in disguises. It aims to provide any disguise imaginable! Leapy Longnoser, the owner, sells objects that seem "real" but are really imitations. Her motto: "If it's not phony, it's not worth it!"

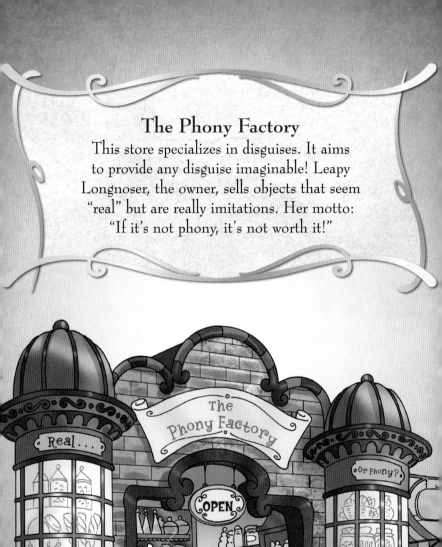

Solution on page 576

Can you find
where the
gorilla costume
is hiding?

FLOWER FAIRY

"I'm looking for a—" I began. But before I could explain about the **VAMPIRE** costume, Leapy Longnoser began running around the shop hurling costumes at me.

"How about a *flower fairy dress*? It comes with a rose crown and a magic wand! Or what about this miner gnome costume, with the fake

MINER GNOME

beard, pickax, and barrel of gold?" she offered.

I shook my head. "I'm looking for a —" I tried again.

Leapy kept on jabbering away. "You

SWAMP MONSTER

might like this **SWAMP MONSTER**

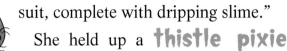

suit, complete with dripping slime."

She held up a **thistle pixie** costume next. "I like this one, but it's a little itchy. Or what about a **Merlin the Magician** tunic? The wand gives off shooting **SPARKS**!" she gushed.

THISTLE
PIXIE

I was beginning to think we'd never get out of there when Spitfire yelled, "Ma'am, we are in a big rush! All my friend needs is a **VAMPIRE** disguise! Now, please hurry!"

MERLIN THE MAGICIAN

hurry
hurry
hurry
hurry
hurry

FACE POWDER, WIG, AND DENTURES!

eapy HUFFED. "Well, why didn't you say so? You need to speak up for yourself, mouse!" she scolded, pulling out a costume.

Cough! Cough!

1

I powdered my snout with face powder . . .

Mmmm . . .

2

. . . and I put on the wig and fake teeth . . .

"Try this one," she said. "It's my best **VAMPIRE**."

I POWDERED my face to look paler. I put on a wig and some fake pointy **teeth**. I sprayed some cologne called **Nightmarish Nights** and put on a three-piece suit and a velvet cape. I put a vial of fake blood in my pocket. Then I looked at myself in the mirror.

. . . and I put on a suit and sprayed myself with some Nightmarish Nights cologne!

I looked like a real vampire!

"Eek!" I looked just like a real **VAMPIRE**!

Spitfire put on a tiny vampire costume, too, and asked Leapy if she had some kind of vehicle a vampire might use.

"How about a **GOLDEN** carriage, lined with *red velvet* and pulled by three horses as black as **INK**?" she proposed.

Spitfire nodded. "Great! And we also need some expensive-looking **gifts** that are actually phony."

Leapy brought out a pile of fake objects, including a fake golden crown, a chest of fake **JEWELS**, and a fake bouquet of flowers. The objects looked so real, it was hard to believe they were phony!

Now there was only one problem. The price for

The Phony Factory

A *fake* gold crown

A *fake* velvet and *fake* silk cloak

A *fake* silver chest

A *fake* marble clock with a *fake* mother-of-pearl face

Fake porcelain plates decorated with *fake* gold, *fake* silverware, and *fake* crystal glasses

A chest of *fake* jewels

A bouquet of *fake* flowers

A *fake* certificate of *fake* royalty

all that was three thousand golden coins!

THREE THOUSAND GOLDEN COINS?!

Where would we get that kind of money? Spitfire had an idea. He took the heavy **GOLD** chain he wore around his neck and gave it to Leapy. The chain had a large sᴘᴀʀᴋʟɪɴɢ ruby dangling from it.

"Will this be enough?" he asked.

Leapy's eyes widened. "It's a done deal!" she cried happily.

Leapy was so thrilled with the necklace that

she decided to throw in some parting gifts. She gave us thirty giant **T-bone steaks**.

Steak for the wolves . . .

"Use these to feed those hungry wolves," she advised.

She also gave us **GARLIC** to stuff in our pockets. "That place is crawling with vampires! And not the phony kind!" she warned.

I climbed into the carriage on **shaky** paws.

. . . and garlic for the vampires. Yikes!

Rancid rat hairs! I wished we were headed home to Mouse Island!

FANG COUNTY: HOW BAD COULD IT BE?

We headed toward Fang County, home of the Vile Vampires. *How bad could it be?* I thought. I leafed through *The Legendarium* to pass the time. Oh, that was not a good idea!

The book said that no traveler had ever made it back from Fang County alive! **NIGHTMARISH** thoughts ran through my head as the carriage **SWAYED** frighteningly. My vampire teeth *rattled* in my mouth. I began to feel carriage-sick.

Meanwhile, packs of wolves raced after us. I tried not to look but couldn't stop myself. The wolves' **BEADY EYES** seemed to bore holes in the carriage.

FANG COUNTY

1. Iron Mountains
2. Gory River
3. Blood Drop River
4. Sweet Blood River
5. Bad Blood River
6. Howling Forest
7. Vampiric Plains
8. Fang Peak
9. Long Wing Wasteland
10. Blood-Sucking Abyss
11. Vampire Lagoon
12. Vampire Castle

The water in Fang County is the color of blood because it contains a lot of iron, which comes from the Iron Mountains.

FANG COUNTY

Fang County, the home of the Vile Vampires, borders the Redswamp Principality to the north, the Dukedom of Scarletfever to the east, the Territory of Terror to the south, and the Land of Sweetblood to the west. It is governed by Count Vampirat IV, a descendant of the famous King Fangsy, the founder of the dynasty.

The Vile Vampires speak an old dialect known as Fanganese, which makes words sound like they are being howled.

For example: "How are youuuuuuuuuuu?"

Fangor coin

The vampires use gold coins known as Fangors, which have Count Vampirat's face on them.

KING FANGSY

DEADSY

SIR SLURPER

DREADSY

BLOODZILLA

COUNT VAMPIRAT

FAMILY TREE

GUEST ROOM (WHERE GERONIMO STILTON SLEEPS!)

THE THOUSAND-STAIR TOWER

VAMPIRAT'S COFFIN COLLECTION

VAMPIRE CASTLE

Built by King Fangsy, Vampire Castle is a nightmarish place. The gloomiest room, reserved for special guests, is at the top of the very steep Thousand-Stair Tower!

VAMPIRAT AND BLOODZILLA'S ROOM

FANGETTA'S ROOM

PORCH WITH A CEMETERY VIEW

FRIGHTFUL FISH AQUARIUM

RECEIVING ROOM

RASPBERRY BUSHES

BALLROOM

THRONE ROOM

FAUXBLOOD PRODUCTION LABORATORY

ENTRANCE TO THE CASTLE WITH A HOWLING BELL

As we drove on, the landscape became **GLOOMIER AND GLOOMIER**! Spiny, leafless trees extended their dry, crooked branches toward the sky. The mountains were **PURPLE**, and the rivers were **RED** like blood.

Every once in a while, Spitfire threw a steak out to the wolves so they would leave us alone. Weren't they supposed to be howling at the moon, anyway? An unsettling **FOG** fell around us. Then it began to rain, and scary **LIGHTNING** flashed in the sky. I wrapped my cape up to my snout. What was next? Killer bees? A tornado? Monstrous alien cats?

Finally, a castle appeared. We had arrived at

VAMPIRE CASTLE!

THE DOORBELL
WAS A SCREAM!

pitfire pulled the reins. The horses reared upward, stopping in front of the castle.

It was made of gray stone, with a black shingle roof. The **flag** that waved on the tower had a vampire bat on it! Just looking at the flag made my whiskers *tremble* with fright. But before I could run away screaming, Spitfire flew out and rang the doorbell.

"**AAAAAAAAAAAHHHHHHH!**"

I jumped. The doorbell was a **SCREAM**!

The door burst open, and a **VAMPIRE** dressed in a butler's uniform appeared. "Whoooo dares to knock at the dooooor of Vaaaaaaampire Caaaaastle?" he called.

"I am Sir Spitfire!" Spitfire yelled. "Please advise **COUNT VAMPIRAT** that the Grand Duke Vampironimo of the **Ratblood** Dynasty has arrived!"

I stumbled out of the carriage and put on my best vampire face. Of course, I had no idea what my best vampire face should look like. So I just tried to stand **TALL** and not swallow my fake teeth.

"I wisssssh I had known you were coooooming," the butler replied. "I would have prepared a weeeeeelllllcoming paaaaarrrrty!"

Spitfire pretended to look surprised. "You didn't

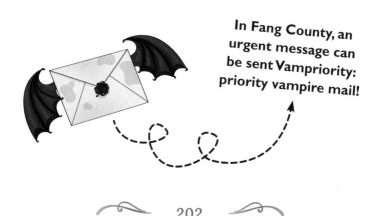

In Fang County, an urgent message can be sent Vampriority: priority vampire mail!

receive my message? I sent it **Vampriority**," he insisted.

The butler shook his head. Then he yelled to his staff, "Prepare the Roooom in the Thousand-Stair Tooooowwwwer! We have a bluuuueee-blooooded guest!"

At the word *blood*, all the servants began licking their lips.

SLURP!

The butler led us down a LONG, **dark** hallway lit with torches. The FLICKERING LIGHTS made the whole place look sinister. Oh, where was a bright chandelier when you needed one?

 WHAT A GLOOMY CASTLE!

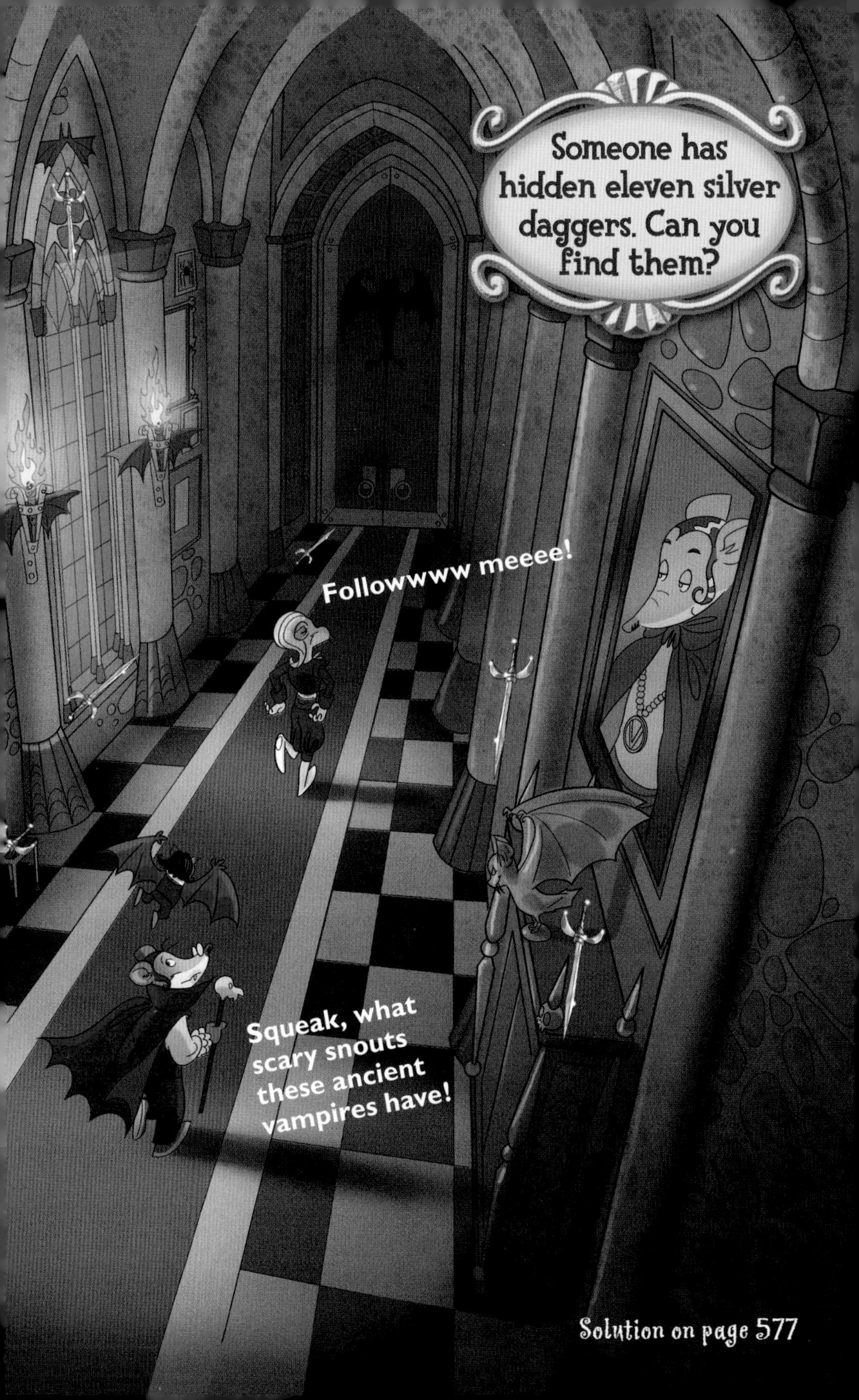

Solution on page 577

THE VAMPIRE COURT

BARON VON BLOODBELT

MADEMOISELLE BATELLA

DUKE DEADBEARD

COUNT VAMPIRAT

COUNTESS BLOODZILLA

CHEF VAMPIREF

FANGETTA, THE DAUGHTER OF THE COUNT

FANGER, THE SON OF THE COUNT

BLOOD BEATS ALL!

e ended up in an enormouse room with a **silver bat throne** at one end and a fireplace at the other. Above the fireplace, the motto of the Vile Vampires was inscribed: **Blood beats all!**

On the throne sat a pale gray rodent wearing a gold medallion stamped with the letter **V**. Gulp! It was ***Count Vampirat***!

Weaving through a cluster of gossiping vampires, the vampire butler strode into the room and announced, "May I present to youuuuuuu the Grand Duke **VAMPIRONIMOOOOOOOO**!"

Vampirat looked me up and down, from my whiskers to my tail, with a penetrating stare. His eyes were so cold, it felt like the temperature in

the room had dropped from **chilly** to **frozen solid**.

"Grand Duuuuuuke Vampironimooooooooo, I presuuuummme . . ." he said in a voice like **thunder**.

I coughed. "Ahem, yes — that is, I mean . . ." I stammered.

Spitfire flew to my aid. "Yes, Grand Duke Vampironimo is of the noble Ratblood Dynasty!" he lied.

Vampirat huffed. "Never heard

Count Vampirat
Count Vampirat loves playing chess, dancing, and dueling with his sword. He bets on everything. He would also do anything to find a noble spouse for his daughter!

Fauxblood
Fauxblood is fake blood. It looks real, but it's actually a juice made from special red raspberries that are exclusively grown in the extensive garden of Vampire Castle.

of thisssss dynastyyyyy."

Right then I was offered a **CUP** of red liquid. "Have some tassssty aged Fauxblooooood," said the vampire.

My stomach lurched.

Luckily, before I could

Cup of aged Fauxblood

Ummm . . .

Drink, Grand Duuuuke Vampironimoooo!

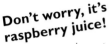

Don't worry, it's raspberry juice!

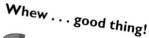

Whew . . . good thing!

faint, Spitfire whispered, "Don't worry, it's not real blood. It's just *raspberry* juice!"

I was so relieved, I chugged down the juice in one gulp and let out a big burp. Oops! How embarrassing!

Vampirat told us he would see us at dinner. As we were leaving, I noticed a little bat wearing a **purple** dress and a bonnet spying on Spitfire. "See you at dinner, Sir Spitfire," she said, giggling before flying off.

It was Fangetta's lady's maid, and her name was Mademoiselle Batella!

Spitfire stared after the bat with a dreamy expression. "Wow! Did you see her? I think I'm in love!"

I smiled at Spitfire.

AH, LOVE!

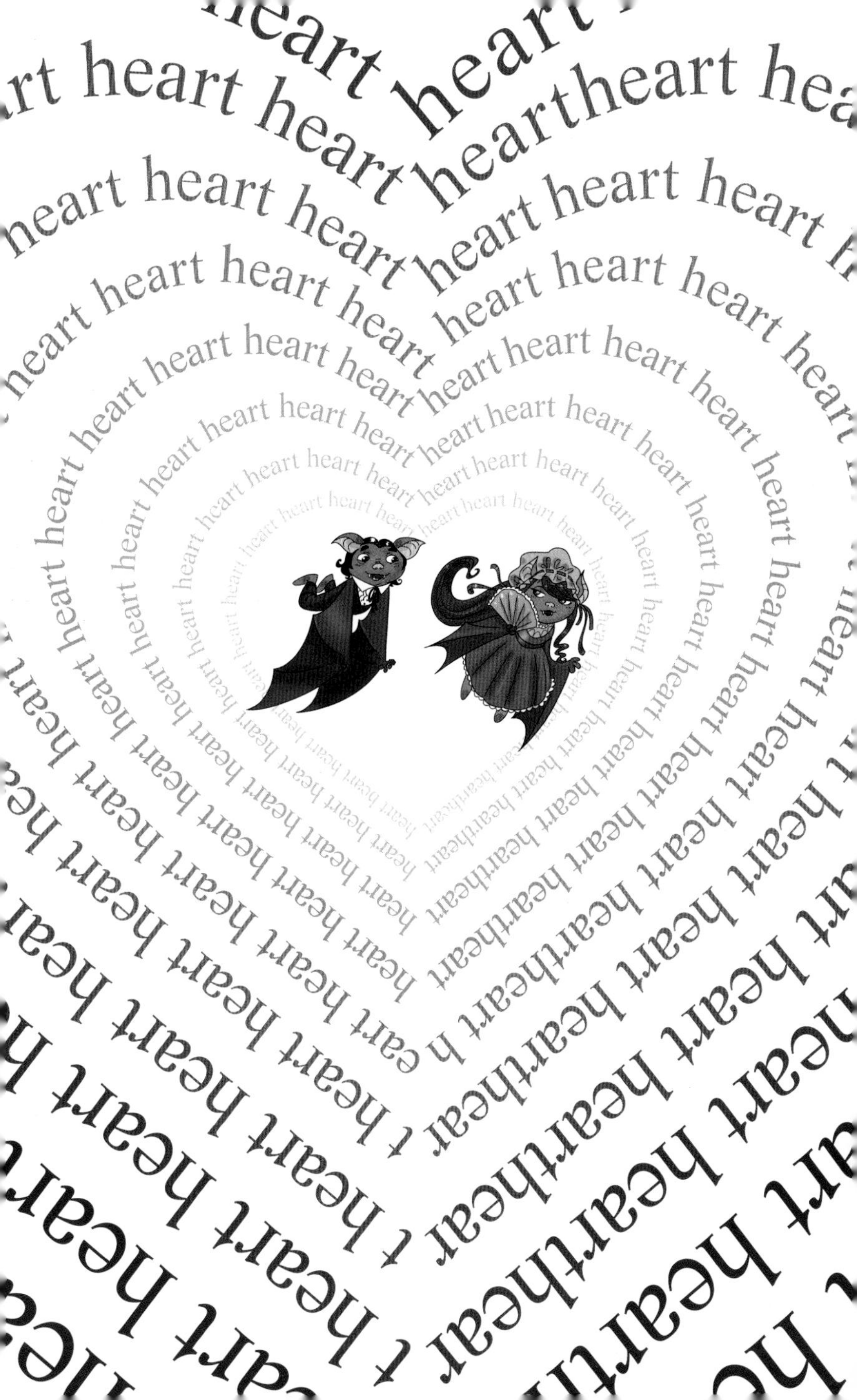

A Thousand Stairs?

he vampire butler led us down a gray **ROCKY** hallway that was dripping with moisture . . .

drip *drip* **drip** *drip*

When we reached a **STEEP** staircase, he passed me his candleholder. "Please proceeeed that way to your rooooom. It's in the tower, just throoooough the thousand-stair labyrinthhhhh," he advised.

I cringed. **A THOUSAND STAIRS?** I could **barely** last five minutes on the StairMouseter at the gym!

I huffed and puffed up the never-ending stairs. About seven thousand years later (give or take

THE THOUSAND STAIR LABYRINTH
MANY CAN ENTER . . .
. . . BUT FEW KNOW HOW TO LEAVE!
Seeee you at dinnnner!
A thousand stairs?!

HELP GERONIMO THROUGH THE LABYRINTH!

Solution on page 577

a few thousand), Spitfire and I arrived at a **NIGHTMARISH** room . . .

The carpet was **RED** with the crest of the Vile Vampires woven into it. The canopy bed had dreary **RED** velvet curtains and (you guessed it!) **bloodred** sheets! Squeak!

On the walls were pictures of **CEMETERIES**. Holey cheese, these vampires needed a new interior decorator!

Then I turned on the water in the bathroom. It spouted a **RED LIQUID**!

"Spitfire, is that— is it b-b-blood?" I stammered.

"No," he assured me.

"It's just water from the Iron Mountains."

Even so, I broke down in sobs.

"I can't do it! I can't pretend to be a vampire!" I wailed.

Spitfire put his wing around me. "Of course you can, Knight," he said. "Just remember to file your teeth every morning, and when you hear the word *blood*, lick your lips and make a **SLURPING** noise!

For those sensitive sorts: The water from the faucets is red because it contains iron from the Iron Mountains.

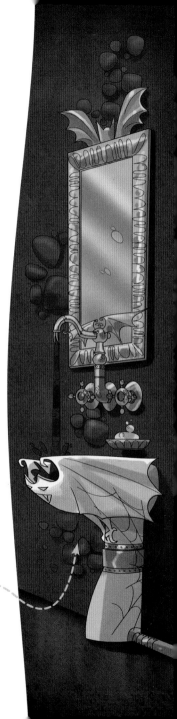

How many ghost
eyes are spying on
Geronimo?

Solution on page 577

I WANT TO MARRY
THAT VAMPIRE!

I pulled myself together and went down to dinner. Spitfire passed out the GIFTS we had brought from the Phony Factory. Luckily, no one noticed they were all fake!

The CROWN went to Count Vampirat, the chest of JEWELS went to his wife, and the other gifts went to the different vampires of the court.

I offered a bouquet of fake red **roses** to Fangetta and made up a poem, "*For you who tends to fascinate . . . a bouquet of roses to celebrate!*"

Fangetta **batted** her eyelashes at me and said, "Oh, thank you, Grand Duuuuke Vampironimooo! By the way, are youuuu ssssssssingle?"

Caught off guard I muttered, "Um, well, yes, I am."

BIG MISTAKE. I watched in horror as Fangetta ran over to Count Vampirat. "I want him, Daddy! I want to marry that vampire!" she insisted, stamping her foot.

Oh, why did I have to be such a **charming** vampire?

The count waited until we sat down at the dinner

For you . . .

Ohhh!

table before he grilled me on my background. "So, Grand Duuuuke Vampironimoooooo, **WHERE** issss your duuuuukedom located? And **HOW MUCH** land do youuuuu have? And how preciousss are your treasuuuuuressss? But most of all . . . how *noble* are your orrrrriginnnnns?"

They all stared at me with curiosity. I muttered, embarrassed, "Umm, I am extremely noble. Well, I mean — that is, my family, from what I remember, dates back to . . . a lot of years ago . . ."

Thankfully, Spitfire piped up. "The Grand Duke Vampironimooooo is so noble that if you cut him, *blue blood* would come out!"

At that moment the vampire cook arrived to serve us dinner, and the vampires began **SLURPING** up their disgusting food.

What a horrific menu! If only I could have ordered a  pizza without attracting too much attention!

MENU

VAMPIRE APPETIZER

VAMPIRE SOUP

VAMPIRE SANDWICH

VAMPIRE ICE CREAM AND POISONOUS BERRIES

The only thing I could eat was the vampire soup. It was the color of blood, but it was actually just **TOMATO** soup!

The conversation was mostly about **GLOOMY** things like **GHOSTS**, monsters, gravestones, and terrible tragedies. Oh, how frightening!

At one point, one of the **VAMPIRES** began telling **jokes**. Can you guess what they were about? Yep, all things **DARK** and spooky!

What a nightmare!

NIGHTMARE!
NIGHTMARE!
NIGHTMARE!
NIGHTMARE!

VAMPIRE SOUP RECIPE
Ask an adult to help you!

INGREDIENTS

4 ripe tomatoes
1 red pepper
1 onion
1 clove of garlic

1 tablespoon olive oil
salt and pepper
2 cups hot water
1 cube vegetable
bouillon

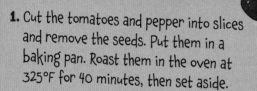

1. Cut the tomatoes and pepper into slices and remove the seeds. Put them in a baking pan. Roast them in the oven at 325°F for 40 minutes, then set aside.

2. Separately, sauté the onion and garlic in olive oil in a pot, then add the roasted tomatoes and peppers. Cook, stirring often, for a few minutes. Add salt and pepper to taste.

3. Blend everything together in a blender until it becomes a puree, and return to pot.

4. Dissolve the bouillon in two cups of hot water. Add to the pot. Cook until the soup is heated through. Enjoy!

VAMPIRE JOKES

QUACK! QUACK!

Q: What has webbed feet and fangs and says "Quack! Quack!"?

A: Count *Duckula*!

VAMPIRE FUN FACTS

Q: How do vampires get clean?

A: They wash in the *bat* tub!

Q: What is the closest that two vampires can be?

A: Blood brothers.

NIGHT LIGHT!

Q: How many vampires does it take to change a lightbulb?

A: Zero! They like the dark.

VAMPIRE SPORTS

Q: Where does a vampire water-ski?

A: On Lake *Eerie*!

Q: What kind of ship does a vampire own?

A: A blood vessel!

OUT TO EAT . . .

Q: How does a vampire like his steak cooked?

A: Bloody!

A CHILLING NIGHT!

It is a dark and stormy night. A rodent misses the last bus and must walk home. The street is dark. He hears a noise and turns to see that Count Dracula is following him!

The mouse starts running away, but soon finds himself at a dead end. Dracula catches up to him. The mouse reaches into his pocket to see if he has any kind of weapon to protect himself. But all he can find is a throat lozenge. He holds it out to the vampire and squeaks, "This throat lozenge will stop your coffin!"

LONELY VAMPIRE . . .

Q: Why does the vampire have no friends?

A: Because he's a pain in the neck!

Aaahh! What nightmarish jokes!

DONE IN THE SUN!

Q: What is something that a vampire will never use?

A: Sunscreen!

I WILL NEVER SSSSSSELL THE CRYSTAL COFFFFINNNNN!

At last, the dinner was over, and Vampirat offered to show me his antique coffin collection. I was thrilled out of my fur! Finally, I would get to see the CRYSTAL COFFIN — the whole reason I set off on this SCARY mission!

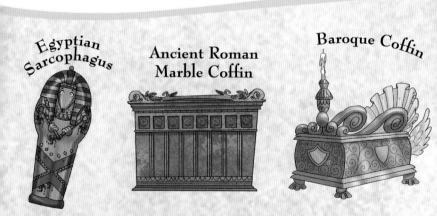

Egyptian Sarcophagus

Ancient Roman Marble Coffin

Baroque Coffin

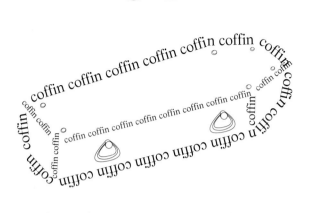

Vampirat brought me to a room with over one hundred coffins. There, he proudly pointed out the CRYSTAL COFFIN. It was decorated with precious stones and lined with **PURPLE** silk. There was a riddle written on the lid . . .

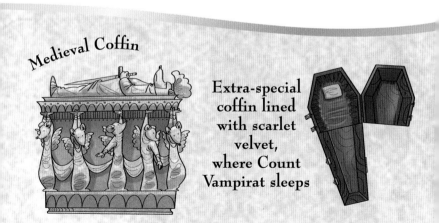

Medieval Coffin

Extra-special coffin lined with scarlet velvet, where Count Vampirat sleeps

I read the mysterious riddle:

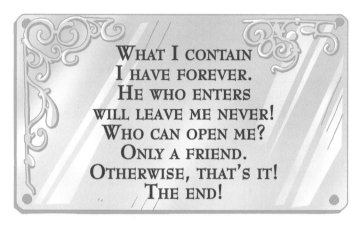

WHAT I CONTAIN
I HAVE FOREVER.
HE WHO ENTERS
WILL LEAVE ME NEVER!
WHO CAN OPEN ME?
ONLY A FRIEND.
OTHERWISE, THAT'S IT!
THE END!

I moved closer, but the count held up his paw. "Beware! Thisssss coffin is **DANGEROUSSSS**!"

I cleared my throat. "Um, well, I was wondering, is this coffin . . . perhaps, er, by chance . . . for sale?" I asked.

The count's eyes opened wide as he thundered,

"NOOOO! I WILL NEVER SSSSSSSELL THE CRYSTAL COFFINNNNNNN!"

THE CRYSTAL COFFIN

Long, long, long, long ago, the Wizard of the West asked the Gnomes of Ash, who live in the Volcano of Fire, to build a Crystal Coffin for him that had magical powers. He wanted to use it to imprison his enemies.

The Crystal Coffin was made using rock crystal and the most precious stones.

It is one of the most mysterious and dangerous objects in the Kingdom of Fantasy.

Right then I came up with a plan. I remembered hearing that the count loved to place bets. So I asked him to make a bet on the coffin. If I won, I got the CRYSTAL COFFIN. If he won, then I would marry his daughter, Fangetta. The count agreed.

Then I had nightmares all night. *What had I done?!*

Daughterrrr, prepareeeee yourrrr weddingggg dressss . . .

Daddyyyyy, try to win! I reallllly like thisss Grand Duuuuke . . .

tossed and turned and tossed and turned and tossed and turned
Poor me!
You can do it!

COUNT VAMPIRAT: TEN!

hen I woke up the next morning, I looked like I'd been pummeled by Furhammed Ali, the boxer! My fur was **STICKING** up, and I had two dark and swollen eyes.

"Well, at least you don't have to put on any powder this morning," Spitfire joked. "You already look like a **SICKLY VAMPIRE**!"

I found out that the first part of the vampire challenge was a **CHESS GAME**.

Everyone whispered, "Whoooo playssss better chesssss, Count Vampirat or the Grand Duke Vampironimooo?"

I sat down at the chess table with the count, and we began to play. Let me just say, it's not easy to play chess with vampires **breathing**

1
THE CHESS MATCH

down your neck!

The count was a pretty decent player. But, luckily, I'd been on the chess team in school. In the end, I managed to get **checkmate**!

The whole court began applauding after I won. The count silenced them with an ICy stare. What a SORE LOSER! Still, I wasn't about to give the count a lesson in sportsmouseship!

Next, he challenged me to a waltz contest. The count danced with Countess Bloodzilla, and I had to dance with (you guessed it!) Fangetta!

The count's daughter clung to me like a vine, batting her eyelashes and cooing, "Here comes the briiiiiide! All dressssssed in redddd!"

Unfortunately, I have no sense of rhythm. I tripped and STUMBLED all over the dance floor.

Oh, why did I have to have two left paws?!

2
THE WALTZ COMPETITION

The vampire judges held up their scorecards. *Count Vampirat: Ten! Grand Duke Vampironimo: Negative Five!*

"Don't worry," Spitfire consoled me. "You have one more challenge! You can still win!"

Sadly, the third part of the challenge was a **DUEL**! Let's just say, dueling isn't exactly my thing. Something about the **jumping** and the swords and the lunging and the . . . did I mention the **swords**?

Anyway, where was I? Oh, yes, the count grabbed his sword and shrieked, "En garde, Vampironimooo! If you **WIN**, you get the coffffin! But if you **LOOOOOSE**, you must marry my daughter immeeeediately!"

Then we began the duel.

The count **ATTACKED** me, and I retreated farther . . . and farther . . . and farther . . .

Before long, Vampirat and I found ourselves

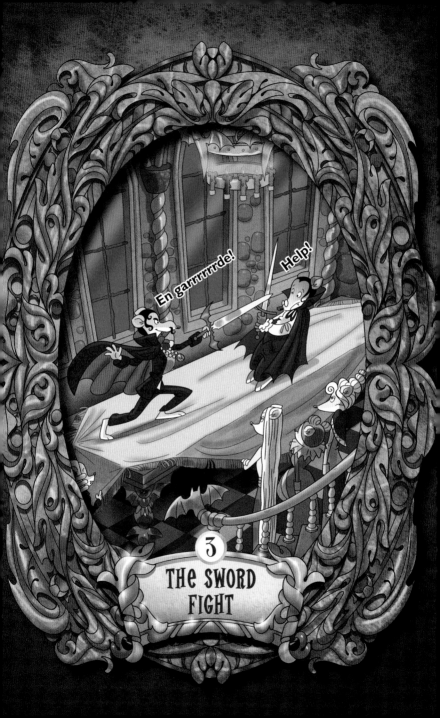

on top of a **LONG** table in the Reception Room. And that's when it happened. The sword slipped from my paws, flew into the air, and cut the CORD that was holding the heavy chandelier! The chandelier **crashed** on top of Vampirat. He was out like a light!

When the count came to, he shook my paw. "You won, Vampironimoooo! Nicccce maaaaaatch!"

WILL YOU BE MY
BEST VAMPIRE?

thanked the count. I guess he wasn't such a sore loser after all. Then I said good-bye to Fangetta and tried not to **smile** too much. After all, she didn't know I wasn't really a vampire and liked to **SLEEP** during the night.

"Ready to go?" I asked Spitfire after we **WRAPPED** up the Crystal Coffin.

The bat coughed. "Um, Knight, I have some news. Batella and I have decided to get **MARRIED**! And, uh, I was wondering . . . will you be my best mouse — I mean, best vampire?"

Of course I agreed! So, at midnight, Spitfire

246

and Mademoiselle Batella united in **matrimony**. He gave her his ruby bat **ring**. She gave him a locket with her portrait in it.

It was a **MARVEMOUSE** ceremony. Those two bats were so in love! I couldn't keep from smiling — though I had to be careful that my **fake fangs** didn't pop out of my mouth!

Mademoiselle Batella

Batella is a descendant of the noble Battellica line of the Long Wing Bats. She speaks seven languages, plays the lute, and collects precious fans. For seven years, she has been the lady's maid for the young countess Fangetta.

When the **WEDDING** was over, I said good-bye to Spitfire and Batella.

The vampires of the court helped me load the Crystal Coffin onto the carriage. Then I began the

Whaaaat a gloomyyy partyyyy!

long **JOURNEY** back to Enchanted City.

My bat friend's last words to me were "Knight, you did it! You can finally relax!"

Oh, if only that were true . . .

HALT! WHO ARE YOU?

When I reached CRYSTAL CASTLE, I took off my vampire disguise and put my bark armor back on. I headed for the front door, but two Knights of the Dark Tower ~~BLOCKED~~ my path.

"HALT! Who are you and what do you want?" they cried.

"I am Sir Geronimo of Stilton, and I have completed my mission," I squeaked.

Suddenly, a group of **dark fairies** arrived. "How did you make it back *alive*?" they shrieked. I started to explain, but they waved me off.

"Whatever. The queen has a new mission for you. You're to bring her green hair from the **three Hairballs** who live in Hairy Woods!" they ordered.

Feeling dejected, I unloaded the CRYSTAL COFFIN out of the carriage and slunk away with my tail drooping. Where was my hero's welcome? When would **Blossom** be satisfied?

Still, I had promised my LOYALTY to the queen long ago. I couldn't give up now.

And so I prepared to leave again, this time to get the green hair from the three Hairballs. Yuck!

The Green Hair from the Three Hairballs

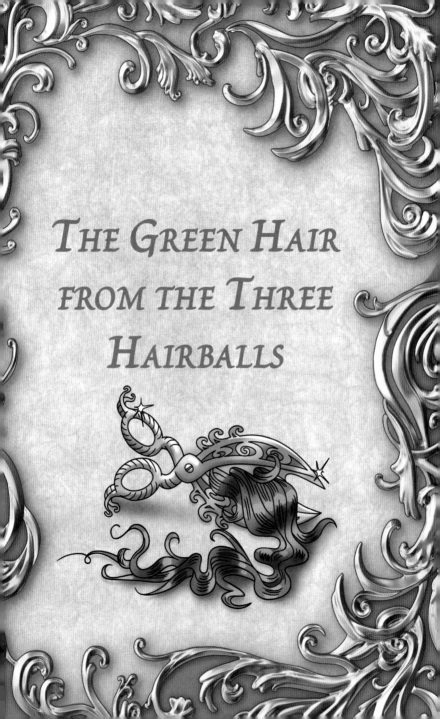

ONE TICKET
TO HAIRY WOODS!

I leafed through *The Legendarium*, looking for the mysterious **HAIRY WOODS**.

Holey cheese, it was really far away!

Lucky for me, the **KINGDOM OF FANTASY TRAIN** passed right through those parts . . .

I headed to the Enchanted City train station. But when I arrived, I realized that I didn't have money to pay for a ticket!

Rats!

Suddenly, among the crowd of magical creatures, I noticed a MYSTERIOUS traveler wearing a BLUE cloak with a hood over his eyes.

He walked over to me and whispered, "Pssst! Mouse, it's me — your friend BLUE RIDER."

Ready?

Yippee!

We **hugged**. I was so happy to see a friend!

"I've been following you for a while," Blue Rider said. "I brought you a few things that might **come in handy** on your next mission."

Then he gave me his cape, his armor, and a bag of gold.

Blue Rider
Geronimo met Blue Rider during his sixth adventure in the Kingdom of Fantasy. Together, they reunited the Royal Sapphire and the Royal Ruby, restoring harmony to the kingdom.

Here, take my armor!

Thank you, Blue!

"Thank you, Blue!" I said. Aren't friends the best?

I watched as Blue Rider DISAPPEARED into the crowd.

I ran to the ticket counter. The ticket clerk, who was a dormouse, was snoring away. Zzzzzzzzzzz!

"One ticket for the next train to Hairy Woods, please," I said.

A ticket to Hairy Woods, please!

Zzzzz! Zzzzzz! Zzzzz!

The mouse opened his eyes. "Just one way?" he snuffled.

"No, I need a **RETURN** ticket," I said.

The dormouse huffed. "Not everyone makes it back from **HAIRY WOODS**, you know. My fool cousin Drowsyfur went a while ago. All that made it back was a package of BONES. Ah, well. You win some, you lose some!"

"I'm hoping to ret-t-t-turn," I stammered.

"Just trying to save you money," the dormouse replied, before dozing off again. *Zzzz!*

By the time I boarded the train, I was already

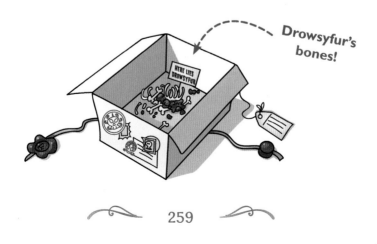

Drowsyfur's bones!

panicking. Still, I remembered what my great-aunt Ratsy always said: "Knowledge is power." So I flipped open *The Legendarium* and read about the Hairballs of Hairy Woods.

Cheese sticks! Hairy Woods was a DISTURBING place! The Hairballs had magic hair that was stronger than steel. How would I ever take any?

Before I could figure it out, the train stopped and the conductor yelled, "HAIRY WOODS stop! Get off if you want, but good luck getting baaaaaaaaaaaaaaaaaaaaaaaaaaaaaaaaaaaaaaaaaaaaaaaaaaaaack!"

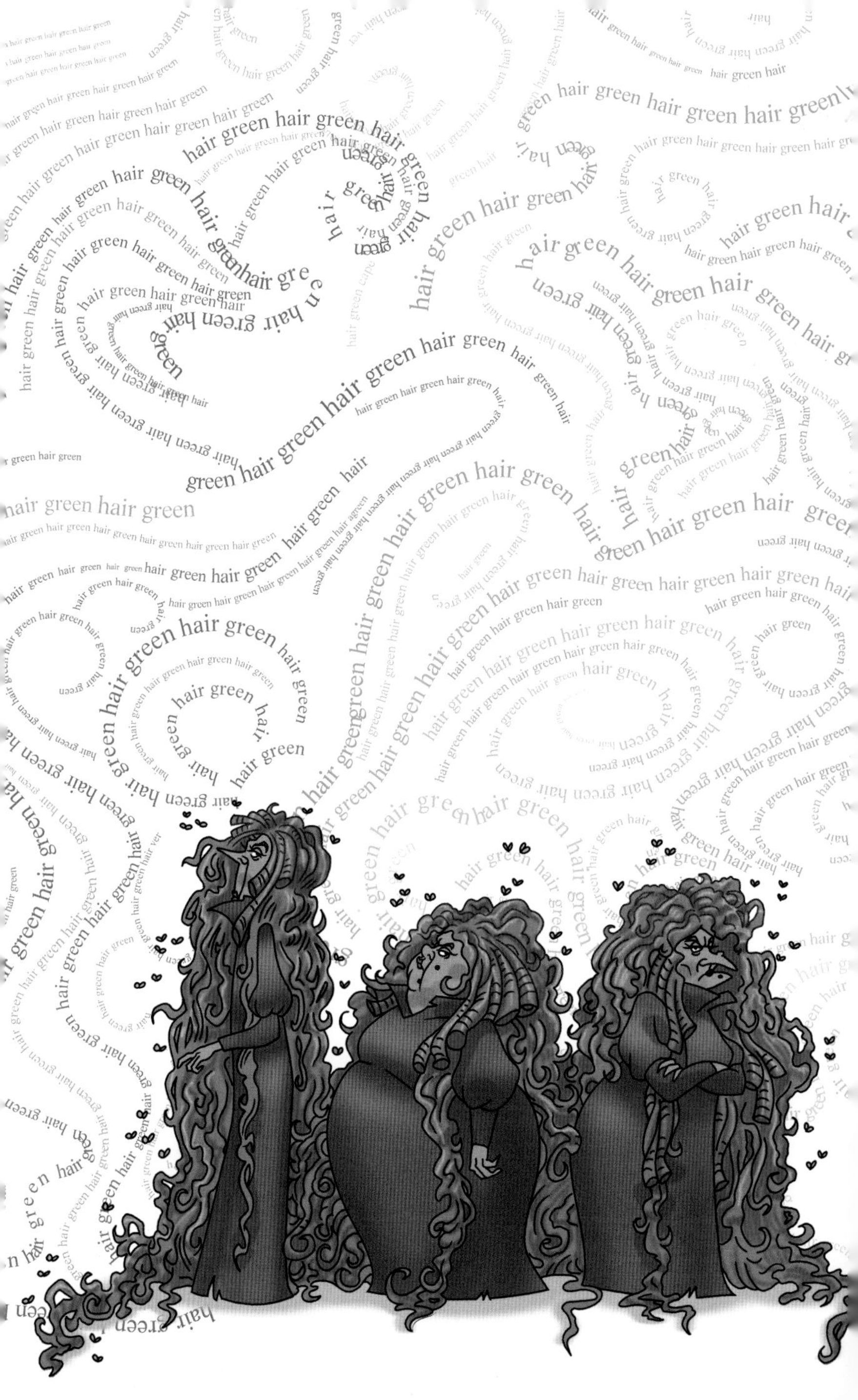

Hairy Woods

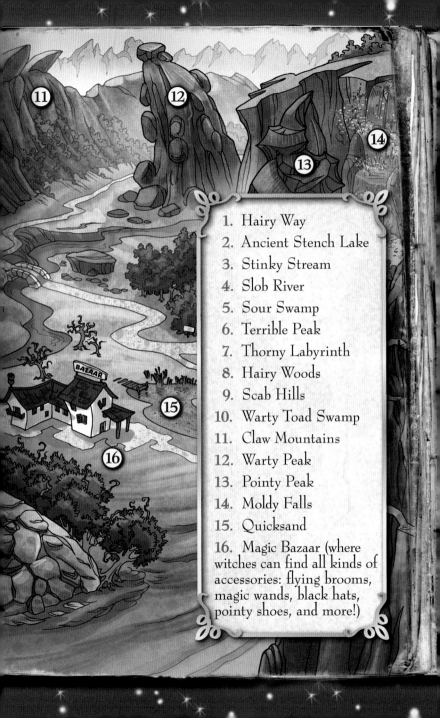

1. Hairy Way
2. Ancient Stench Lake
3. Stinky Stream
4. Slob River
5. Sour Swamp
6. Terrible Peak
7. Thorny Labyrinth
8. Hairy Woods
9. Scab Hills
10. Warty Toad Swamp
11. Claw Mountains
12. Warty Peak
13. Pointy Peak
14. Moldy Falls
15. Quicksand
16. Magic Bazaar (where witches can find all kinds of accessories: flying brooms, magic wands, black hats, pointy shoes, and more!)

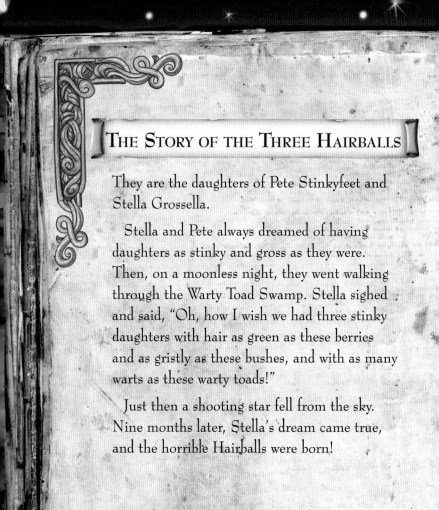

THE STORY OF THE THREE HAIRBALLS

They are the daughters of Pete Stinkyfeet and Stella Grossella.

Stella and Pete always dreamed of having daughters as stinky and gross as they were. Then, on a moonless night, they went walking through the Warty Toad Swamp. Stella sighed and said, "Oh, how I wish we had three stinky daughters with hair as green as these berries and as gristly as these bushes, and with as many warts as these warty toads!"

Just then a shooting star fell from the sky. Nine months later, Stella's dream came true, and the horrible Hairballs were born!

THE MAGICAL GREEN HAIR

The Hairballs each have green hair that is long, curly, and stronger than steel. The Hairballs love their hair so much they haven't cut or washed it since they were born!

Moldylocks,
the smelliest

Coldylocks,
the coldest

Oldylocks,
the eldest
(she was the first
to arrive!)

THUMP! THUMP! THUMP!

I was the only traveler to get off at the Hairy Woods station.

A sign **POINTED** the way to the **THORNY LABYRINTH**.

I wandered through the labyrinth until I saw strange tracks on the ground and heard a noise that sounded like someone running.

THUMP! THUMP! THUMP!

I hid behind a tree and saw a house made of bones ahead of me. It had claw windows, a roof covered in skulls, and a door made of sharp teeth that snapped open and shut. Snap! Snap! Snap!

But the most extraordinary thing was that the house was moving! And not just moving a little — it JUMPED here and there on CHiCKeN LeGs, complete with feathers and all! I waited for the house to tire of jumping and then I approached . . .

ENTRANCE

The Thorny Labyrinth

Solution on page 577

HELP GERONIMO THROUGH THE LABYRINTH!

Snails are crawling away everywhere. How many are there?

Solution on page 577

STILTONSTYLE, WE NEED THE WORKS!

As quiet as a mouse, I approached the window to peek inside. **Ugh!** It's a good thing I hadn't eaten lunch recently. If I had, I would have lost it! Seriously, I hate to be mean, but those Hairballs were beyond **filthy**!

Clouds of fleas and gnats swarmed around their long, curly, **rotten** green hair. And their dirty long nails looked like claws.

BLECHHH!

As they brushed their greasy manes, the three Hairballs sang a SONG in piercing voices . . .

THE THREE HAIRBALLS' SONG

OUR HAIR IS TOUGH,
BUT OUR CURLS LACK
SPRING.

A LITTLE GREEN DYE
WOULD ADD SOME
ZING!

BUT HAIRDRESSERS
NEVER WANT TO STAY.

WHO KNOWS WHY
THEY ALL RUN AWAY!

That's it! I thought. Now I knew how I would get near that hair. I would pretend to be a hairstylist!

A hairstylist's coat . . .

1

1 I took Blue Rider's cloak and made it into a hairstylist's coat.

2 I made a mustache out of roots and glued it on with some pine resin.

. . . a mustache . . .

2

3 Then I put together a **WIG** made of bark!

Finally, I knocked on the door of the Chicken Feet House.

. . . and a wig!

3

"Good day, my name is **GERRY STILTONSTYLE**. I am a hairstylist!" I said.

The Hairballs stared at me with **WIDE** eyes as I continued. "Ahem, I was just passing through Hairy Woods, and I thought I might see if there were any **beautiful** clients out here . . . who, um, wanted to become more **beautiful**. I do manicures and makeup, too."

Immediately, the three Hairballs pulled me

Ack!

Come here!

into the house and locked the door.

The first witch screeched, "Stiltonstyle, **we need the works**! Shampoo, dye job, blow out, and some of those hot **curlers**!"

The second Hairball added, "We want manicures, too. Rotten green nail polish for all three of us. It's all the rage, right, girls?"

The third witch shrieked, "And we want you to do our makeup: green **BLUSH**, green **MASCARA**, and green **LIPSTICK**. We need to look **BEAUTIFUL** or . . .

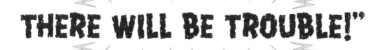

THERE WILL BE TROUBLE!"

WE WANT OUR MANICURES!

Comb, brush, scissors, soap

Olive oil and eggs

Spinach paste

The Three Hairballs put some water on the **FIRE** to heat it up. They poured the water into three giant barrels.

"Work your magic, Stiltonstyle!" the oldest Hairball ordered. "Beautify us!"

I gulped. Forget magic, it would take a miracle to beautify these three!

Still, I had to try. First, I washed their hair with **soap**. Then I made a conditioner out of **olive oil** and **EGGS** . . . and finally,

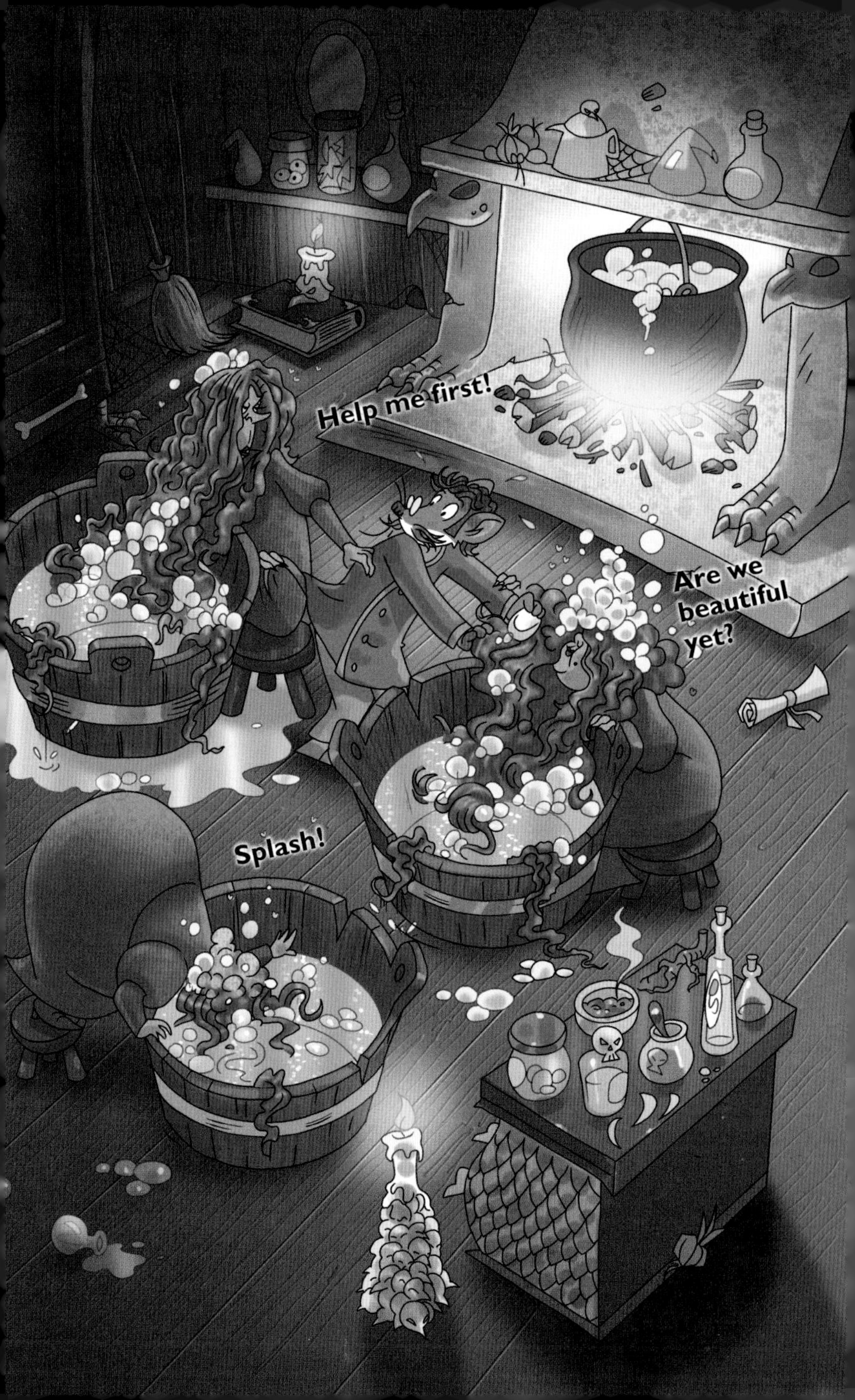
Help me first!
Are we beautiful yet?
Splash!

Flying Broom
This mode of transport is common among Hairballs, but quality flying brooms are rare: The best ones are made of elder wood and come from the faraway Elderwood Forest!

Flyola, the
Flying Broom

a spinach paste to brighten up the green in their hair.

Then I blew their hair dry, praying I wouldn't blow off my mustache and blow my cover!

As I worked, I noticed a WOODEN BROOM whimpering, "Oh, woe is me. If only I knew my way home. I'm so sick of these Hairballs!"

Just then one of the Hairballs piped up. "I heard that, you **rotten** stick of wood! You better

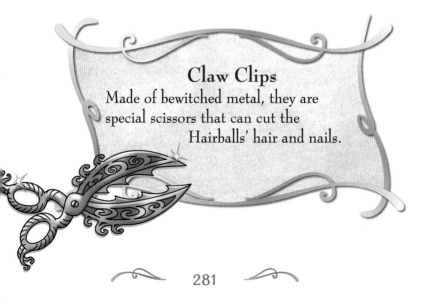

watch what you say or you'll end up a pile of ash in the fire!"

The broom muttered under her breath, "One of these days I'll **ESCAPE**. If only I had a friend . . ."

I have a map, I thought. Maybe I could help the broom find her way home.

"WE WANT OUR MANICURES!" the Hairballs cried, interrupting my thoughts.

Claw Clips
Made of bewitched metal, they are special scissors that can cut the Hairballs' hair and nails.

The Hairballs' Horrible Makeup

Roach Eye Shadow

Stinky Rotten-Sewer Deodorant

To cut their nails, I had to use the Hairballs' pair of **CLAW CLIPS**. They are magical scissors so strong they'll cut through nails as thick as claws.

After their nails were cut, I tried suggesting haircuts. "Short hair is so **IN** right now. You'd

Before the makeover . . .

Green Slug Saliva
Lipstick

Mummy
Face Powder

Scorpion Venom
Mascara

be the envy of all your friends," I coaxed.

But the Hairballs flew into a **RAGE**.

"𝕟𝕠 𝕨𝕒𝕪!" they shrieked. "We love our long **GREEN** locks! Besides, we don't have any friends!"

I sighed, dejected.

How would I ever complete my mission?

. . . and after the makeover!

SNIP, SNIP!

 worked on the **Hairballs** late into the evening. I did my best, but they certainly wouldn't be winning any beauty pageants.

Fortunately, the Hairballs seemed very satisfied with their new looks.

Moldylocks praised me, "Well done, Stiltonstyle! You really gave it your all!"

Goldylocks proposed, "You're hired! From now on, you can take care of our precious hair and all our styling needs!"

Oldylocks showed me to the guest room. "Sleep now, Stiltonstyle. At dawn, you can give us toning facials with swampy mud!" she concluded.

That night, I pretended to sleep. I waited until the Hairballs were *snoring*, then I left the guest room.

It was then that something BRUSHED against my paw.

A tiny voice whispered, "It's me, Flyola, the flying broom! I decided to make a break for it, but I don't know my way around Hairy Woods. Maybe we could leave together!"

"Sure," I replied. "But first I have to do something. You see, I need to get ahold of some

of the Hairballs' **HAIR**, because I have to bring it back to Blossom. She sent me on this mission and —"

The broom cut me off. "Love to hear the story, but we need to fly. If those Hairballs wake up, we're done!" she *hissed*.

Then she **WRIGGLED** out the window, whispering, "Hurry up!"

I grabbed the Claw Clips and crept into the Hairballs' bedroom on tippy-paws. Their terrible snoring filled the room . . .

I approached the first Hairball's bed.

SNIP, SNIP, SNIP! I CUT OFF HER HAIR!

It was so long!

Then I approached the second bed.

SNIP, SNIP, SNIP! I CUT OFF HER HAIR!

It was so thick!

Then I approached the third bed.

SNIP, SNIP, SNIP! I CUT OFF HER HAIR!

It was so hardy!

Clutching all the **magic green hair**, I turned to leave, but the Claw Clips fell . . . making a horrible racket!

The Hairballs woke up screaming. "Aaaahhh!

BADABAAANGG! Oops!

Who cut our hair?!"

Then they saw me and yelled, "Chicken Feet House, stop that stylist!"

FLYOLA was waiting for me impatiently. I grabbed Blue Rider's helmet, **jumped** out the window and onto the broom, and in a flash we were up in the air.

It was then that I made an **AWFUL** discovery. I had no idea how to drive a flying broom!

Oops!

Help!

Where are the brakes?

THAT WAY, FLYOLA!

Eventually, I got the hang of it, and I managed to stay STEADY on the broom (well, sort of steady). Far below us we could hear the Hairballs calling after us in a furious rage. The Chicken Feet House jumped up to try to **BITE** us. And claws came out of the windows to try to **grab** us!

But it was too late. We flew high into the sky, which shone with the last stars of the night.

"Which way to Enchanted City?" asked Flyola.

Remembering the map in *The Legendarium*, I said, "That way, Flyola. Keep left, toward the

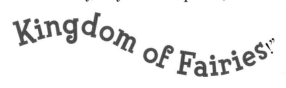

As we flew, Flyola told me her story.

How many
little leaf fairies
are following
Geronimo and
Flyola?

Toward the Kingdom of Fairies!

Solution on page 578

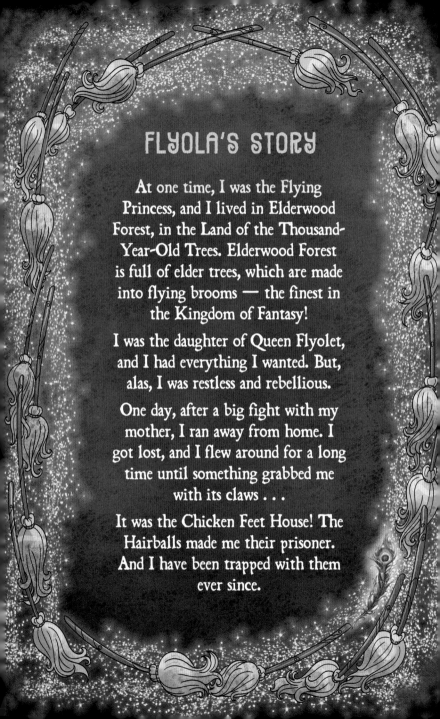

FLYOLA'S STORY

At one time, I was the Flying
Princess, and I lived in Elderwood
Forest, in the Land of the Thousand-
Year-Old Trees. Elderwood Forest
is full of elder trees, which are made
into flying brooms — the finest in
the Kingdom of Fantasy!

I was the daughter of Queen Flyolet,
and I had everything I wanted. But,
alas, I was restless and rebellious.

One day, after a big fight with my
mother, I ran away from home. I
got lost, and I flew around for a long
time until something grabbed me
with its claws . . .

It was the Chicken Feet House! The
Hairballs made me their prisoner.
And I have been trapped with them
ever since.

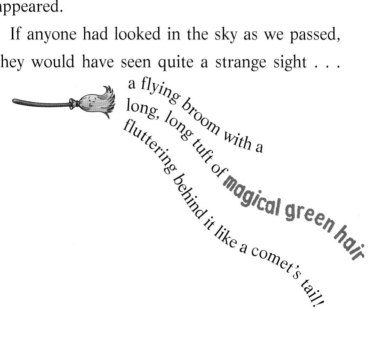

She concluded, "So, Sir Knight, after taking you to Enchanted City, I will go **home**. I can't wait to see my mother and tell her I am sorry!"

We flew and flew and flew

until stars disappeared and the first rays of sun appeared.

If anyone had looked in the sky as we passed, they would have seen quite a strange sight . . .

a flying broom with a long, long tuft of *magical green hair* fluttering behind it like a comet's tail!

THE RETURN TO ENCHANTED CITY

The next evening, we landed in **Enchanted City**. I thanked **FLYOLA** and gave her a piece of Blue Rider's cloak to remember me by.

"Thanks," Flyola said with a **smile**. "And now I have something for you." With that, she began

That blue looks great on you!

Thanks!

shaking her head back and forth as if she had a terrible itch. Then she waved good-bye and flew off.

Moldy mozzarella! Had the broom picked up **lice** at the Chicken Feet House?

But when I looked down, I realized Flyola had shaken all the stardust she had picked up on the flight into a small pile for me. How sweet!

I gathered the **shiny** dust in a piece of cloth and headed once more to Crystal Castle.

Before I even reached the castle, a black crow

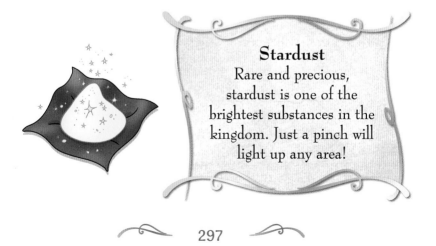

Stardust
Rare and precious, stardust is one of the brightest substances in the kingdom. Just a pinch will light up any area!

Caaaaaaww!

BONK!

flew over me and dropped a small box on my head. **BONK!**

Inside the box was a scroll from **Blossom** with a message written in the Fantasian Alphabet.

"Hey, you, Knightsy!" the crow cawed. "I am Cawsby, **NEFARIA'S** assistant. Queen Blossom wants you to give me the green hair, and then to bring her the **treasure** that is described on that scroll."

Ouch!

BONK!

NEFARIA

TO TRANSLATE THE MESSAGE YOURSELF, YOU CAN FIND THE FANTASIAN ALPHABET ON PAGE 575. OR YOU CAN FIND THE MESSAGE IN ENGLISH ON PAGE 578.

I sighed. Would I ever survive this never-ending story? Still, I didn't know what to do but keep going. I wrote to Blossom to tell her I was up for the new mission.

Then I left Enchanted City again. This time I was searching for something called the **STONE MASK**.

As I walked, the wind carried the crow's last words . . .

IF YOU WANT SOME FREE ADVICE, GO BACK WHERE YOU CAME FROM!

THE AIR HERE IS NO GOOD! CAAAWWW!

THE STONE MASK

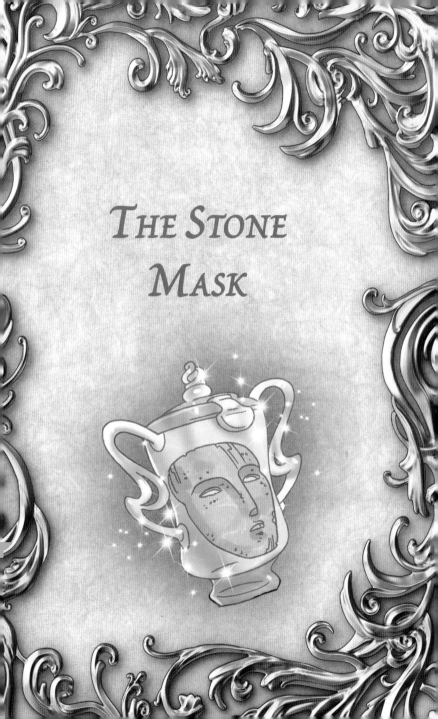

THE SECRET OF THE STONE MASK

I took a break and *leafed* through *The Legendarium*. Reading about the **STONE MASK** brought back so many memories!

Squeak! The Kingdom of Nightmares was so scary!

Cackle, the queen of the witches, was holding Blossom prisoner there . . .

I had found the Stone Mask during my third voyage to the Kingdom of Fantasy.

Here's what happened: Cackle, the queen of the witches, kidnapped Blossom and took her to the Kingdom of Nightmares. **GRIM**, the king of nightmares (and also Cackle's half brother), reigned there. He wore the **STONE MASK**,

Grim challenged Cackle to a duel . . .

Then he took off the Stone Mask, which split in two!

and it made him evil! But once he met Blossom, his heart softened.

Grim challenged Cackle to a **DUEL** to free Blossom, and he won. The Stone Mask split in two, and the king of nightmares became good. Blossom was free! She and Grim had fallen in **love** in the process, and they got married. He changed his name from Grim to George.

Later, **Blossom** realized that the two pieces of the **MYSTERIOUS** mask kept

joining
back
together.

So she gave the mask to her uncle, the wizard **Lakeness**. Lakeness lives in Wave Castle, a water castle built on the bottom of the Shining Waters Lake.

THE STONE MASK

Nema the Faceless Witch originally
made the Stone Mask out of granite
from Desperation Mountain.
Whoever wears it immediately
becomes evil!

The mask broke in
half when Grim won
the duel, but its magic
was so powerful that it
continued to join itself
back together, as if it had
its own will. So Blossom
sent the mask to be watched
over by the wizard Lakeness, in the Shining
Waters Lake, where the sun never rises and
never sets.

I closed *The Legendarium*, my whiskers trembling with worry. If the Stone Mask was in a castle at the bottom of a deep lake, how would I ever get it? *Glub!*

HOLD ON TO MY FINS!

After a day and night of walking, I reached the mysterious **LAND** near the . . .

SHINING WATERS LAKE.

I walked along the shore, staring at the **WAVES**. How would I get to the bottom of that lake?

Note to self: Next time, pack scuba gear! But wishing things were different wouldn't change my situation.

Suddenly, I saw the most heartbreaking sight. An enormouse fish was trapped in a tangled net.

The fish was as WHITE as the purest snow. He had bright, sparkling blue eyes and the most spectacular **golden** fins. Oh, how those golden fins shone!

"Please, traveler! Can you help me?" the poor fish called, FLAILING DESPERATELY.

The net was thick, and I could see the sadness in the fish's gaze.

"I will help you!" I called.

Without a second thought, I grabbed the NET and ripped it to shreds. The golden fish was . . .

FREE!

The Golden Fish

The fantastical golden fish has an amazing singing voice and is more than a thousand years old! Through the centuries, he has grown bigger, and his golden fins have grown thicker, making them extremely valuable. He is constantly being chased by thieves who want to steal his golden fins!

But instead of swimming away, he sang in a beautiful voice,

"Thank you, traveler,
for setting me free!
You are as kind as kind can be.
Now, tell me, sir, what can I do
To help you on your travels, too?"

After explaining to the fish that I was headed for **WAVE CASTLE**, he told me to jump onto his back. Have you ever ridden on the back of a fish? Let me tell you, they are super slippery! I grabbed on to the fish's **fins** for dear life!

Then he dove beneath the waves. Good thing everything is **enchanted** in the Kingdom of Fantasy, and I was able to breathe underwater!

SHINING WATERS LAKE

1. Golden Fish Beach
2. Great Shrimp Ditch
3. Algae Forest
4. Great Carp Rock
5. Big Bubble Peak
6. Reckless Rock
7. Swirly Whirlpool
8. Great Blue Cliff
9. Never-ending Abyss
10. Curlicue Current
11. Road to the Castle
12. Wave Castle

Down, Down, Down . . .

After a little while, I got used to the whole breathing-underwater-while-riding-a-giant-fish thing and **LOOKED** around. We passed a strange rock shaped like a carp. Bubbles swirled all around us. We slipped right by Reckless Rock, even though *The Legendarium* specifically said it was reckless to do so.

Right after the dangerous Swirly whirlpool and before the Never-ending Abyss, I saw . . . the

Curlicue Current!

"Hold on tight!" yelled the Golden Fish. "Down there at the bottom is Wave Castle!"

He dove into the current, which **spun** us around and around and down and down toward the Never-ending Abyss . . .

DOWN DOWN DOWN DOWN DOWN DOWN DOWN DOWN DOWN DOWN DOWN DOWN DOWN DOWN DOWN DOWN DOWN DOWN DOWN DOWN DOWN DOWN DOWN DOWN DOWN DOWN DOWN DOWN DOWN DOWN DOWN DOWN DOWN DOWN DOWN DOWN DOWN

EXIT

The Never-ending Abyss Maze

Solution on page 578

There's Wave Castle!

How many fish are in this picture?

The current left us at the bottom of the lake, where the **darkness** was black as ink. Yep, we had reached the Never-ending Abyss, the place where the **SUN** never rises or sets! The Golden Fish pointed me to a castle made entirely of water.

It was the legendary **WAVE CASTLE**!

WAVE CASTLE

Wave Castle is found at the bottom of Shining Waters Lake. Blossom's uncle, the wizard Lakeness, reigns from the castle. It is made entirely of special magical water that comes from the bottom of the Never-ending Abyss. The water is charged with energy and can be molded to form walls, ceilings, chandeliers, and other objects.

The Stone Mask is hiding inside Wave Castle in a special chest.

WELCOME TO OUR WATERS! BLUB! BLUB!

catfish swam toward us. "Welcome to our waters! **Blub! Blub!**" he said. "Please allow me to accompany you to *WAVE CASTLE*!"

Soon, a whole *school* of fish was escorting

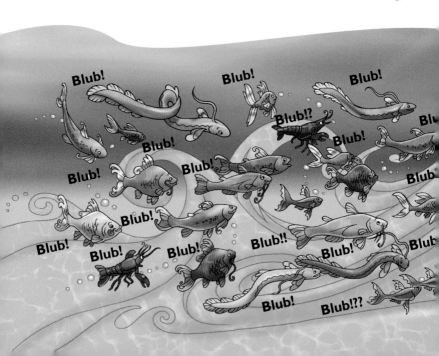

us to the castle. As they swam, I heard them murmuring to each other . . .

"Blub! Can you believe it? It's the mythical **Golden Fish**!"

"Blub! Yeah, but who is riding him?"

"Blub! Is that Sir Geronimo? The **fearless** knight?"

I tried to look strong and fearless. But it wasn't easy. The saltwater was making my whiskers **droop** and my eyes tear. Rats!

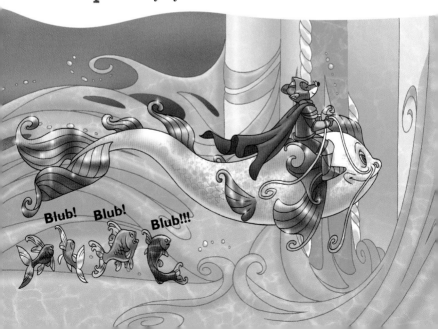

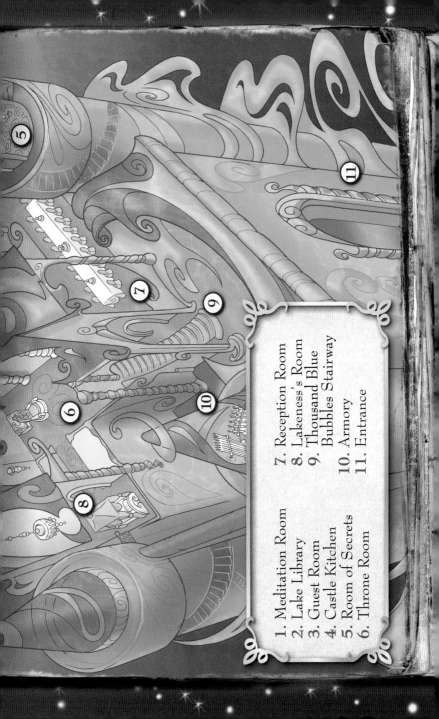

1. Meditation Room
2. Lake Library
3. Guest Room
4. Castle Kitchen
5. Room of Secrets
6. Throne Room
7. Reception Room
8. Lakeness's Room
9. Thousand Blue
   Bubbles Stairway
10. Armory
11. Entrance

When we entered Wave Castle, the whole place was so magnificent that my eyes **popped** out of my fur and rolled away. Okay, okay, they didn't really **ROLL** away, but you get the picture. It was an **incredible** sight! Everything was made of water — the ceiling, the floors, the walls, even the furniture!

Lakeness

The wizard Lakeness is Blossom's uncle. He belongs to the Winged Dynasty, the purest creatures in the Kingdom of Fantasy. His penetrating eyes can read the heart of anyone, and his words are illuminating.

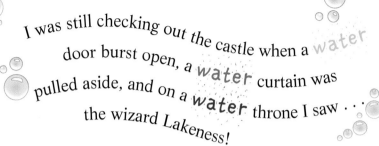

I was still checking out the castle when a water door burst open, a water curtain was pulled aside, and on a water throne I saw · · · the wizard Lakeness!

He had long BLUE hair, and he was wearing an algae tunic decorated with PEARLS and a pointy hat.

"Hello, I am —" I began.

He lifted an EYEBROW.

"I know," he said.

"Um, well, I'm here because —" I continued.

He lifted his other EYEBROW.

"I know," he said.

"Okay, well, I need the mask —"

This time he lifted both EYEBROWS and sighed. "I know you need the mask. What I don't know is why my sweet niece Blossom wants such an EVIL object."

 327

The wizard removed a **chain** from around his neck with seven keys on it. Then he used the keys to unlock SEVEN WATER CHESTS, one by one, each one inside another.

3. The Chest of Kind Generosity

1. The Chest of Healthy Goodness

2. The Chest of Exquisite Sweetness

The Seven Chests of Virtue

The seven chests of virtue were built by the fairies to hold the Stone Mask. To combat the evil of the mask, the fairies infused their infinite goodness in every chest and gave each one the name of a virtue.

One, two, three, four, five, six . . . when Lakeness had opened the last chest, I gasped. There inside, floating in a vase of water, was the **STONE MASK**!

4. The Chest of Kind Compassion

6. The Chest of Supreme Wisdom

7. The Chest of Delicate Sweetness

5. The Chest of Swift Hope

The Stone Mask

MORE DANGEROUS
THAN A SCORPION!

he wizard gave me the vase. I took it with trembling paws. What a **shock**! No, I don't mean I was surprised. I mean that the vase gave me an **ELECTRICAL SHOCK**! Talk about negative energy!

"Don't worry, Knight," said the wizard. "You are **FEARLESS**, which means this mask cannot harm you."

Twisted cheddar rolls! I guess now wasn't the time to mention I'm not really fearless. I am a real scaredy-mouse!

"Just be careful," the wizard continued. "The mask is an evil object. Please go immediately to CRYSTAL CASTLE and give it directly to my niece. Remember, what you are carrying is more **DANGEROUS** than a scorpion, more poisonous than a rattlesnake, and more deadly than a hot dog at the Salty Sea Shanty. Have you ever eaten there? Ugh!

"Anyway, whatever you do . . .

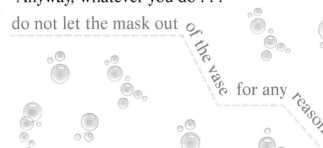

do not let the mask out of the vase for any reason!"

Lakeness stroked his beard. "I must tell you, Knight, I am very **worried** about Blossom," he said. "She hasn't been herself lately, and I don't know why she would want the **STONE MASK**. But I must respect her wishes."

Clutching the vase, I said good-bye to the wizard and climbed back onto the Golden Fish. He swam in **silence** back toward Crystal Castle.

I couldn't wait to get rid of that creepy **STONE MASK**. But when we reached the castle, a

sign on the door read
CLOSED!

Even though the sign
said it was closed, I
KNOCKED on the door
anyway.

"What do you
want?!" a nasty
voice shrieked.

"Ahem, it's

Did you try knocking?

No one is answering!

CLOSED!

Huh?!

What a mystery!

Sir Geronimo . . ." I began.

A **CLAWED** hand shot out from behind the door, and the voice ordered me to hand over the mask. I did, and in return, the hand passed me a scroll with Blossom's seal on it.

"The queen has written the name of the **TREASURE** that you must now bring her. This is your next mission!" ordered the voice.

Then the door **SLAMMED** shut on my snout. I unrolled the scroll and translated the words that were written in the Fantasian Alphabet.

When, oh when, oh when would this adventure *END* *END* **END**?

To translate the message yourself, you can find the Fantasian Alphabet on page 575. Or you can find the message in English on page 578.

334

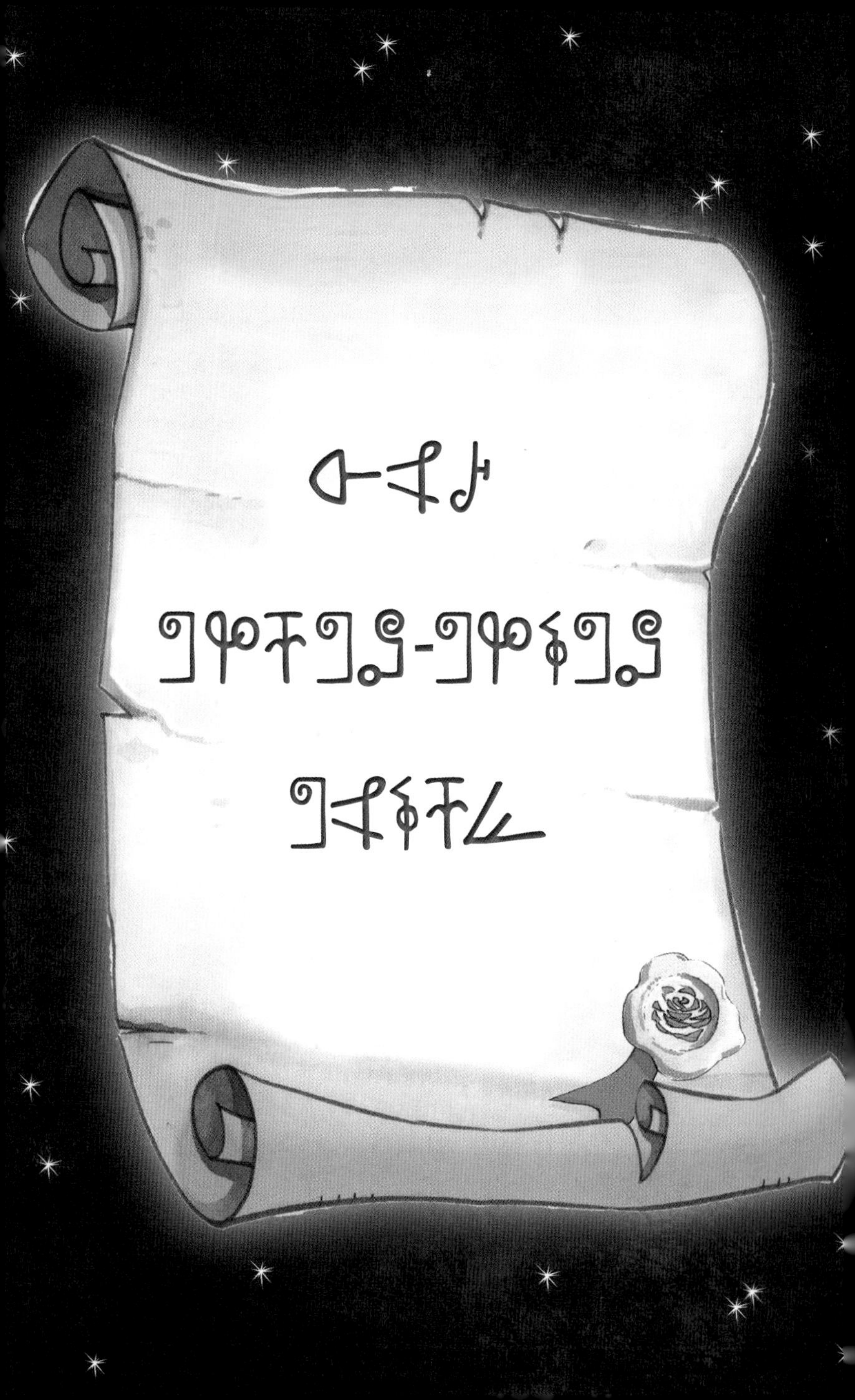

I left the castle and walked away with my whiskers drooping. The wizard was right — Blossom really was acting strange. But I am a mouse of my **WORD**, and I had agreed to help the queen, so that's exactly what I would do. I just hoped I wouldn't **lose my fur** in the process!

THE CLICK-
CLACK
CHAIN

BADBEARD THE PIRATE

checked *The Legendarium* to figure out where I would find the next treasure. The magical Click-Clack Chain could be found on

To get there, I had to board a ship and follow the Fantastic River, which flowed into the Sea of Mermaids.

From there, it would be a **LONG**, **LONG**, **LONG** trip to Mount Giant. I sighed. I was tired already, but it didn't look like I had time for a quick ratnap.

MOUNT GIANT

Mount Giant is the home of Redhot, the giant fire-breathing dragon. According to legend, this ferocious dragon watches over one of the most precious treasures in the Kingdom of Fantasy: the mythical, magical Click-Clack Chain.

Still, no traveler has ever visited this grave and dangerous land, so many of the details about the chain remain a mystery.

MOUNT GIANT

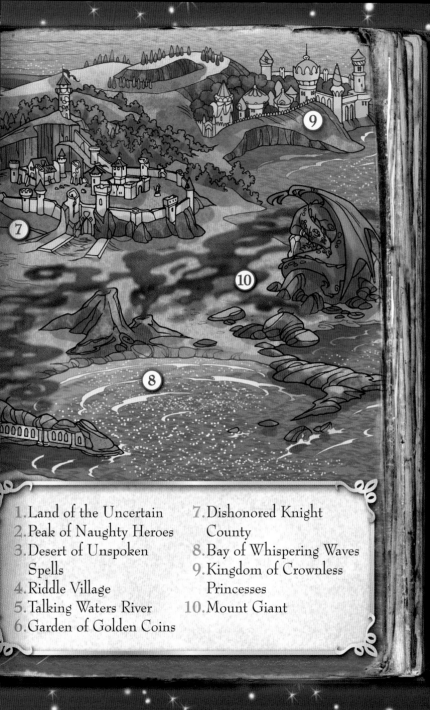

Unfortunately, there wasn't much information about Redhot . . . except that he can breathe **FIRE**! Squeak!

I headed to the port of **Enchanted City** on the shore of Fairy Lake. I needed to find a way to get down the Fantastic River to the Sea of Mermaids.

Down at the port, I found a shabby ship named **The Outlaws**. An evil-looking gnome with a **GRAY** beard eyed me up and down. It

Badbeard the Pirate
After being kicked off *Horizon*, the talking ship (an ally of Queen Blossom), this shady gnome pirate became captain of the ship *The Outlaws*.

was **BADBEARD THE PIRATE**!

"What are you looking at?" the gnome growled.

I thought about pointing out that *he* was the one staring at *me* but decided against it. Picking a fight with a fierce **PIRATE** wasn't a good idea. Instead I said, "I need a ride to Mount Giant."

Badbeard studied me. What was he looking at? My fur, or my whiskers, or my good POSTURE? Turns out, it was none of the above. He was staring at the **armor** Blue Rider had given me.

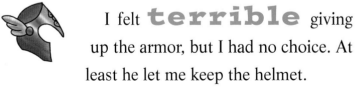

"I'll take the armor, and you'll get a ride," he snarled.

I felt **terrible** giving up the armor, but I had no choice. At least he let me keep the helmet.

In place of the armor, Badbeard gave me an old shirt. I put it on, and we left.

We sailed along the Fantastic River until we reached the Sea of Mermaids.

As we sailed, we saw many **LEGENDARY** lands. In fact, they were so legendary that no one had ever gone there!

Suddenly, we found ourselves in the middle of a storm. My stomach began **rolling** with the waves.

Poor me!

I was so seasick!

We passed scary whirlpools, dangerous rocks, and monstrous **WAVES**!

At last,

we spied

FOGGY

land . . .

Badbeard pointed to the shore. "That should be **MOUNT GIANT**, if the legend is true."

"B-b-but how will I get there?" I stammered.

Badbeard snickered. "If you give me that **silver** helmet, I'll give you a lifeboat. Otherwise, you can swim," he sneered.

With tears in my eyes, I gave him the helmet. Then I got into the †iNϒ lifeboat and headed for shore. The boat TUMBLED over the choppy waves as I rowed and rowed . . .

Heeelp!

THIS WAY TO
REDHOT'S NEST!

uckily, I had the **COMPASS** that Chatterclaws had given me. It helped me find my way through the fog, and I finally reached the shore. *I was alive!*

But where was Mount Giant? To find out, I leafed through *The Legendarium* . . .

I'm alive!

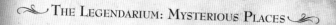

REDHOT THE GIANT DRAGON

Redhot is the largest fire-breathing dragon in the Kingdom of Fantasy. He lives on Mount Giant and spends his days sitting in a silver straw nest while protecting his treasure, the magical Click-Clack Chain. According to legend, at one time Redhot had a wife as large as he is. But, alas, she was kidnapped by the queen of the witches!

I walked along the path, my heart thumping . . .

1 Suddenly, I saw a strangely shaped sign. It read THIS WAY TO REDHOT'S NEST. ARE YOU SURE YOU WANT TO GO? I shivered but kept walking.

Huh?!

THIS WAY TO REDHOT'S NEST. ARE YOU SURE YOU WANT TO GO?

1

2 I continued until I saw a second sign. YOU ARE ALMOST AT THE DRAGON REDHOT'S NEST. LAST CHANCE TO **LIVE**! TURN AROUND! I **gasped** but kept going.

3 Finally, I saw another sign: HALT! YOU HAVE ARRIVED AT REDHOT'S NEST. SORRY, TOO LATE TO CHANGE YOUR MIND. HOPE YOU HAD A GOOD LIFE!

I broke out in sobs. Then I saw a shape so tall it touched the clouds. It was a **giant emerald-green dragon**!

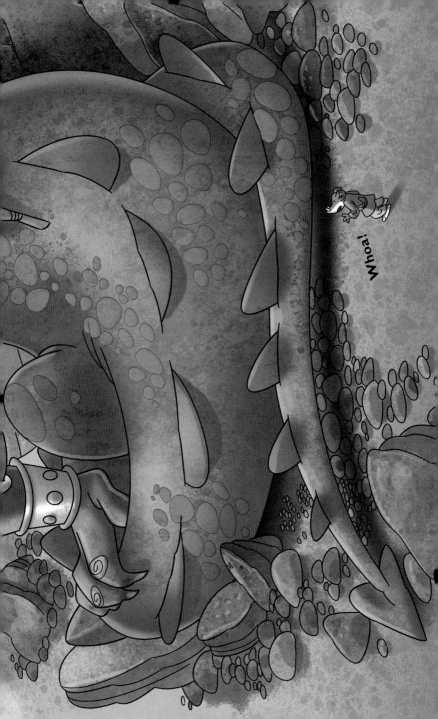

EVEN THE DRAGON'S

FLAMES WERE GIGANTIC!

Oh no! Redhot burned the last pages of The Legendarium!

Labyrinth of Flames

EXIT

Solution on page 578

HELP GERONIMO THROUGH THE LABYRINTH!

YOU SMELL
LIKE A MOUSE!

Luckily, the dragon soon stopped breathing **FIRE**. I hurried to blow out the fire that had started at the back of *The Legendarium*. I stopped the flames, but the last pages of the book were **charred** to a crisp. Oh, how would I tell Scribblehopper I had ruined his precious book?

I was still thinking about the book when a scary voice **thundered**, "Well? Do

Pfff!!

you need something? You didn't come all this way for nothing, did you?"

Like a snake, the dragon slowly **EXTENDED** his neck, and sniffed me. "Mmm,

you smell like a mouse! Are you a mouse?" he asked.

I **trembled**. "Well, yes — um, that is, I mean, I am a mouse, if you don't mind," I babbled.

The dragon licked his lips. "Oh no, Redhot has nothing against mice. He loves mice. He loves them **BOILED**, **FRIED**, *baked*, **STUFFED**, and even raw!" he cried.

I swallowed. Oh, why did I have to admit I was a **mouse**? I could have passed for a hamster. Who knew if the dragon liked them?

Hamsters have much more **fur** after all.

"So, why are you here?" the dragon's voice thundered. "**REDHOT** doesn't have all day! He's got places to go, things to burn . . ."

SHUDDERING, I explained that I had come for the **CLICK-CLACK CHAIN**.

The **dragon** roared. "You want the chain, mouse? Then you must **answer** four

DRAGON RIDDLES!"

THE MOUSE'S RESPONSE

Once upon a time, a gigantic dragon met a mouse. The dragon was starving, since he hadn't eaten in centuries. But though the dragon was big, he wasn't that bright. The mouse, however, was very clever. So before the dragon could devour him, the mouse said, "Oh, enormouse dragon, I know that you will eat me. But I would like to choose how I will die."

The dragon agreed. He said, "Would you like to die by being roasted, or squashed, or ground, or some other way? Tell me, and I will accommodate you!"

The mouse responded . . . and the response saved his life! What did the mouse say?

Solution on page 578

THE TREE OF GNOMES

How many gnome faces are in this tree?

Solution on page 578

2

DRAGON LEGS

Solution on page 578

Look closely at the dragon. How many legs does it have?

A CUP FOR TWO FAIRIES

Look closely at this picture. Do you
see a fancy goblet . . . or the faces
of two fairies?

Solution on page 578

THE GOLDEN EGG
IN THE SILVER NEST

The dragon snickered. "Well, mouse? What is your response? *Redhot is waiting!*"

The riddles made my head spin like a top, around and around and around!

The dragon pulled out an hourglass filled with **GOLDEN SAND**. "When the sand in this hourglass has drained, Redhot needs answers. Got it?!"

I thought and thought and thought. Then I said,

I thought and thought and thought . . .

"**I've got it!** I have the solutions!"

One after another, I told the answers to the dragon.

DID YOU SOLVE ALL THE DRAGON RIDDLES? YOU CAN FIND THE SOLUTIONS ON PAGE 578.

Redhot was so annoyed, a little fire shot out of his nostrils. "Oops," the dragon apologized. "Redhot gets **angry** when he doesn't win. But you gave all the right answers, so Redhot will **HONOR** his word."

And with that, the huge dragon raised himself from his silver straw nest. Inside the nest was a solid **GOLD EGG**. Then the dragon broke open the egg. What was inside?

The Click-Clack Chain!

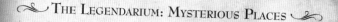

THE MAGICAL CLICK-CLACK CHAIN

The Click-Clack Chain was made by miner gnomes for Dorothy, the queen of the Land of Gold. To make it shiny, the gnomes soaked the chain in a cauldron full of the rays of the sun. They captured the rays with an enormouse mirror in the sun during the summer when the sun is its most intense.

Dorothy gave the chain to the dragon Redhot to protect it. It is a magical chain, and it can bind objects with infinite force. To make it lock, you must say the magic words: "Click-clack, paddywack! Lock up, chain, front to back!"

I stared at the legendary chain sparkling like the rays of the sun were woven into it.

The dragon handed it to me and said, "To make the chain lock around something, just say the magic words:

"Click-clack, paddywack!
Lock up, chain, front to back!"

Ooooh, the chain!

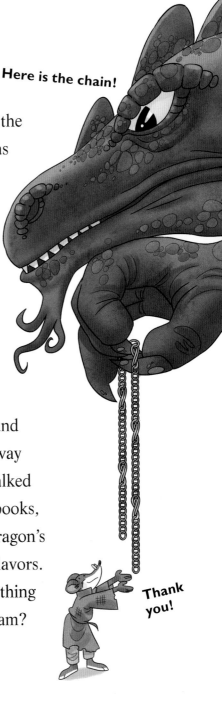

Here is the chain!

I thanked Redhot for the treasure. "**Blossom** has ordered me to bring her this chain," I explained.

"Well, why didn't you say so in the first **PLACE**?" the dragon said with a grin. "Redhot would do anything for the queen!"

After that, the dragon and I began chitchatting away like old friends. We talked about the weather, books, music, and the dragon's favorite ice-cream flavors. Who knew a fire-breathing dragon could eat ice cream?

Thank you!

"Redhot can't get a cone, because of the **melting**," the dragon explained. "Redhot sticks to shakes."

It was then that I noticed the dragon's cheek. It was SWOLLEN.

"Does your tooth hurt?" I asked.

"Who, me? No. Redhot is **TOUGH**. Redhot is strong. Redhot . . ."

A moment later, Redhot began **groaning**. "OW, OW, OWWW!"

REDHOT'S TOOTH HURTS

he dragon winced. "Redhot's **tooth** hurts," he admitted.

"It's okay," I said. "Just open your mouth and I'll take a look."

Of course, I didn't know a thing about teeth. I'm an **author**, not a dentist! Still, the dragon opened his **HUGE** mouth.

Great balls of mozzarella! His teeth were **ENORMOUSE**!

Luckily, I didn't need a medical degree to find the problem. The dragon had a **small bone** stuck in the gums between two of his teeth. So I took my belt, tied

it around the bone, and **PULLED** and pulled until . . . the bone **POPPED** out!

"Thank you, mouse!" the dragon cried. "That **bone** has been stuck for ages, since Redhot ate all those trolls. Trolls are tasty, but they have such pointy bones."

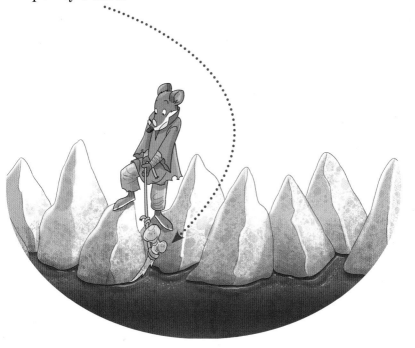

Chamomile flowers

Afterward, I boiled a bunch of **CHAMOMILE** flowers and made a compress to help with the swelling.

Redhot felt much better. He said, "In return, I would like to offer you three dragon gifts . . ."

I feel great!

THE THREE DRAGON GIFTS

1

THE REVERSE MAGIC
WORDS TO UNLOCK THE
CLICK-CLACK CHAIN

2

A DRAGON'S
TOOTH

3

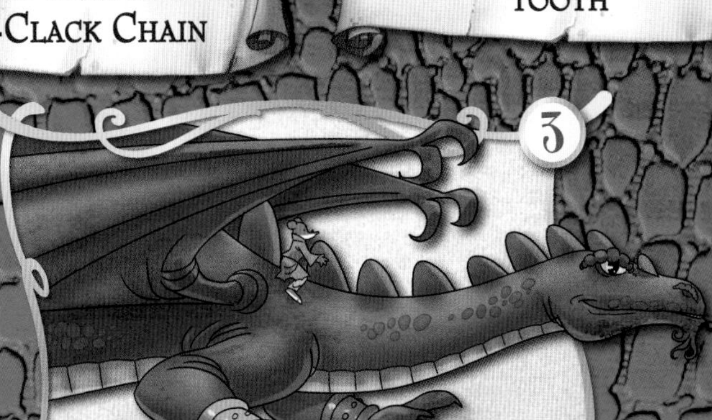

A RIDE ON REDHOT THE
GIANT DRAGON

THE FIRST DRAGON GIFT ...

MAGIC WORDS:
Click-clack, paddywack!
Lock up, chain, front
to back!

REVERSE MAGIC WORDS:
Click-clack, reverse back!
Untie, chain, piddlypack!

Just knowing the magic words to lock
the Click-Clack Chain is not enough. It's
important to also know the reverse magic words
to unlock the chain and undo its binding spell.
Otherwise, you can only use the chain once!

THE SECOND DRAGON GIFT . . .

A DRAGON'S TOOTH!

The dragon's tooth gives courage to even the most fearful. All you have to do is rub the tooth with your right paw, stick out your tongue, stomp your right foot three times while waving your left paw in the air, and then blink both your eyes and wiggle your whiskers!

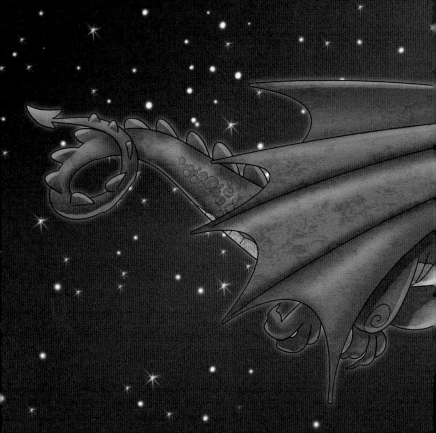

THE THIRD DRAGON GIFT ...

A superspeedy flight ...

...aboard Redhot the Giant Dragon!

THIRTEEN LOCKS!

he dragon flew me all the way to **Enchanted City**. "Good-bye, mouse," he said when we arrived. "Please tell the queen that Redhot is a faithful subject of hers."

Dragon's Tooth

Clutching the dragon's **TOOTH** for courage, I approached the entrance to the castle. It had been replaced with a heavy **iron** door with thirteen **LOCKS** securing it!

I knocked. "I am Sir —"

I hadn't even finished squeaking when a small window opened in the door. A **CLAWED** hand snatched the magical chain. Then the hand gave me a bottle with a top shaped like a tear. "Fill this vial with CONDENSED

 SADNESS. This is your last mission from the queen! Be quick about it!" hissed an evil voice.

I took the vial and saw

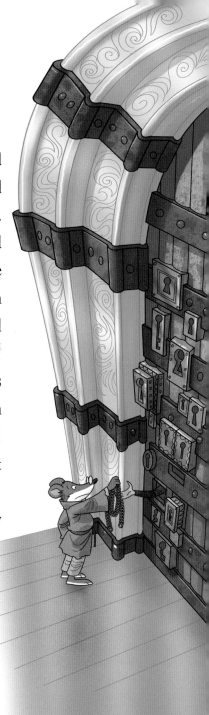

that there was writing etched on the side:

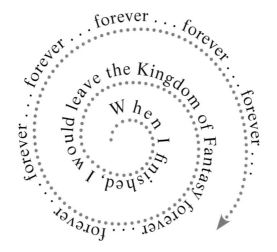

CONDENSED SADNESS

So this was my seventh and last mission.

forever . . . forever . . . forever . . . forever . . . forever . . . forever . . . forever . . . forever . . . When I finished, I would leave the Kingdom of Fantasy forever

CONDENSED
SADNESS

WHAT A SAD, SAD DAY!

left quickly so that no one could see me cry. What had happened to my dear **FRIEND** Blossom? She used to be so kind. Being disappointed by a friend like this was more upsetting than being **attacked** by an enemy.

I sat under a **weeping willow**. Its branches drooped downward and made it seem sad, just like me.

Sighing, I pulled out *The Legendarium* to read about . . .

CONDENSED SADNESS.

CONDENSED SADNESS

Condensed Sadness is made up of the saddest tears of the saddest creature after it's had the saddest experience. Some say that Condensed Sadness is found in the saddest place in the Kingdom of Fantasy: Melancholy Village.

The concentrate makes even creatures that are naturally happy become sad. The effects are immediate and contagious. It is so dangerous, its use is forbidden throughout the Kingdom of Fantasy!

Just one drop of this concentrate will make you extremely sad!

Still feeling sad, I wandered . . . and wandered . . . and wandered . . . and wandered . . .

I wandered until I was outside the city, **in the middle of nowhere**, where a dreary rain was falling. I wandered and wandered until I ended up getting lost in the maze of **HERO CEMETERY**.

MELANCHOLY VILLAGE

MELANCHOLY VILLAGE

Solution on page 579

EXIT

Sir Geronimo of Stilton

HELP GERONIMO THROUGH THE MAZE!

I finally found my way out of the cemetery . . . but not before seeing that there was a **TOMBSTONE** all ready for me!

What a **SAD** feeling . . .
in such a **SAD** place . . .
on such a **SAD** day!

Sir Geronimo
of Stilton

I hid out at the end of the Bridge of Unhappiness next to BITTERNESS RIVER. Nearby was the Fountain of Tears. The water from the fountain came out slowly, **DROP** by **DROP**, so it looked and sounded like tears.

DRIP! DRIP! DRIP!

I bought a bunch of tissues (there was a reason that town had a tissue factory!) and sat on a bench to CRY.

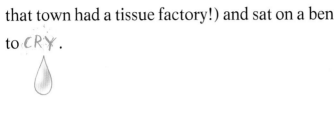

AND CRIED I CRIED AND CRIED I CRIED AND CRIED I CRIED AND CRIED I CRIED

CRIED I CRIED AND CRIED I C
CRIED I CRIED AND CRIED I C
CRIED I CRIED AND CRIED I CRIED AND CRIE
AND CRIED I CRIED I CRIED AND CRIED AND
I CRIED AND CRIED I CRIED AND CRIED I CRIED AND

As evening fell, I had a pile of used tissues next to me, and I was still sobbing.

Suddenly, a thought hit me. I didn't need to go **FAR** to complete my mission. I already had what Blossom wanted.

MY TEARS!

Here is the Condensed Sadness!

My tears *were* the Condensed Sadness because *I* was the saddest creature in the Kingdom of Fantasy, in the saddest place in the Kingdom, at a time when I felt the SADDEST, after going through the saddest experience. After all, what was **sadder** than being abandoned by your friends? Why didn't Blossom like me anymore?

I gathered all my TEARS in the vial and went and left it in front of Crystal Castle.

Then I sat on the steps of the castle and ate the CANDY Boils the chameleon had given me and drank the JUICE from Factual the gnome.

Oh, how I missed my friends!

BE STILL AND LISTEN

Now that I had finished my last mission, I could head back home. But things didn't feel right. I wanted to save my **friendship** with Blossom before I left, but how?

I needed someone to give me a wise answer. I leafed through *The Legendarium* and read about a place called *Wisdom Hill*.

Maybe I'd find an answer at Wisdom Hill.

I started walking, and soon I reached the hill. Atop it was a **STONE** with an inscription on it:

IF YOU NEED A WISE ANSWER, SIT HERE. BE STILL AND LISTEN TO YOUR HEART.

I sat. Have you ever tried to be **still**? It isn't easy. My paws tapped. My whiskers twitched. Eventually, though, I relaxed.

I watched as **dawn** broke over Enchanted City, turning the sky **PINK**.

I waited... and waited... and waited...

IF YOU NEED A WISE
ANSWER, SIT HERE.
BE STILL AND LISTEN
TO YOUR HEART.

I thought about Queen Blossom . . .

I had to save our friendship!

I stood on a rock, snout in air, paws on my hips, feeling strong. (Then I tripped on a pebble and fell, but don't tell anyone.)

A true friendship is worth saving!

A FAKE POISONOUS MUSHROOM!

irst, I needed to come up with a plan. How could I find out why Blossom had changed so much? I decided to investigate in SECRET. To buy a disguise, however, I needed MONEY.

So I took a job as a dockworker, unloading cases of FISH.

By evening, I was in **terrible** pain. Oh, why did I have to drop that case of fish on my paw?!

Argh!

But I had earned three copper coins. I returned to the Phony Factory to find a disguise. **Leapy Longnoser**, the owner, recognized me immediately. "Hey, you're the rodent who bought the vampire costume! What can I do for you?" she asked.

I told Leapy what I needed, and I showed her the three **copper coins**.

"That's it?" she huffed. "Well, for that kind of money, all I can give you is this gnome

Ouch!

costume. It's on sale, but it's a little small and has a **HOLE** in the tights. Plus, there's a button missing on the jacket and it smells **MUSTY**. But it comes with a nice fake poisonous mushroom!"

I tried to get Leapy to give me a different costume, but she refused. "Either

take the gnome or go back home!" she snickered.

I **SHUFFLED** out the door. I looked ridiculous! The costume was way too **SMALL**. I had to walk with my knees bent!

One thing was certain, though: Even **my grandfather** wouldn't recognize me!

Umm . . .

Hee, hee, hee!

A pillow to look plump

WE CAN MAKE
MOUSE MEAT!

ressed as a gnome, I headed back to CRYSTAL CASTLE. But when I reached it, I gasped. The castle had been transformed! Now it was made of **black steel** and was surrounded by a dark and **unsettling** cloud.

I saw a black marble sign:

THIS BUILDING IS NOW CALLED DARK CASTLE!

BY THE DECREE OF BLOSSOM, THE QUEEN OF THE KINGDOM OF FANTASY

Why had **Blossom** done such a thing?

I heard some noises and hid. Then I saw seven stinky **TROLLS** entering the castle.

"Do you think that knight is gone for good?" one asked another. "If not, Blossom said we can make mouse meat out of him!"

THAT MADE ME START TO TREMBLE!

Ack!

Mice taste good!

Yum!

Yum

Yum!

Next, forty-four enormouse roaches arrived. "Guys, if Sir Geronimo is around, we need to tell the Knights of the Dark Tower immediately. There's a **bounty** on his head!"

THAT MADE ME TURN WHITE!

If we see the knight . . . we'll make him into mouse meat!

Then I saw a swamp monster, four *ghosts*, and many other scary creatures pass.

"I hope that knight's gone," one said. "What a Goody-Two-shoes! Now we can be our **rotten**, mean old selves!"

THAT MADE ME START TO SWEAT!

I'm ready . . .

. . . for some . . .

. . . mouse meat!

Snurkle!

Snurkle!

Flap!

Bzzz!

Flap

Gluuub!

Next, three **vultures** arrived, squawking. "Once Sir Geronimo is **dead**, we can gobble up that furry flesh. We haven't had mouse meat in a while. Yum, yum!"

THAT MADE ME FEEL FAINT!

Bzzz!

Tick!

Tick!

Nighty-night, Knight!

Excuse me, has anyone seen my head?

Grk!

Puff!

Bzz!

Puff!

Splat!

Finally, a procession of **witches** arrived, singing. "The knight is at the castle no more. Thank the heavens! He was such a bore!"

THAT MADE ME OFFENDED!

Bye-bye, boring knight!

What a snore . . .

Bzzt!

. . . a party pooper . .

. . . a fool . . .

All the good creatures of the Kingdom of Fantasy watched the scene in horror. "Where is Blossom, our queen? Why is she inviting **EVIL CREATURES** to the castle?" they cried.

I had to get inside the castle to understand what was happening. I rubbed the dragon tooth for courage.

. . . a stick-in-the-mud . . .

. . . a snoop . . .

. . . a busybody!

A minute later, I saw my lucky break. A group of **gnomes** were entering the castle with a cart of strawberries. I joined them like I was part of their group, and the *Knights of the Dark Tower* let us through.

As soon as I was inside, I slipped down a dark hallway.

CHATTING LIKE OLD FRIENDS!

How Crystal Castle had changed! Now the walls, the floors, and the ceilings were all made of **BLACK STEEL**. The carpets, furniture, and **PAINTINGS** were now all black. The black curtains covering the windows did not let in one single **RAY** of sunlight.

I headed down the hallway until I passed Door 12 of the Ceremony Room, where Blossom's **throne** was. The door was open, and I heard Blossom's voice along with another one.

I pressed my face up to the door, and what I saw made me **freeze**.

Blossom was on her throne. At her side I saw . . .

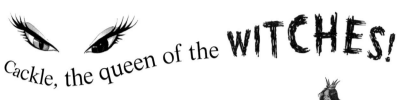

Cackle, the queen of the **WITCHES!**

The queen of the fairies and the queen of the witches were chatting like old friends. **HOW STRANGE!**

But that's Cackle's voice!

I listened to the conversation with my heart in my throat. It went like this:

CACKLE: So, what do you think of the dark fairies?

Blossom: They are the perfect court for me!

CACKLE: And tell me, has the knight carried out all the missions?

Blossom: Yes, all seven!

CACKLE: Was he upset that you treated him badly?

Blossom: Ha, ha! You should have seen his face!

CACKLE: Wait till he **FINDS OUT** our

 SECRET PLAN!

Using all seven treasures, we can imprison her forever!

Blossom: Oh, my dear, when we finish with her, he won't be able to save her anymore. She is finished, and so is the Kingdom of Fantasy!

I listened carefully, scratching my gnome beard.

What was going on?!

Why was Cackle getting along so well with Blossom?

What was the secret plan they had together?

Who was the mysterious "her" they were talking about?

And most of all, why did Blossom seem to hate me so much?

WITHER!

he **evil** laughs of both queens echoed through the Ceremony Room.

Hee, hee!

Ha, ha, ha!

Hee, hee!

Heeeee, hee, hee!

Aaaahh, ha, ha!

Ha, ha, ha,

Hee, hee!

By now, I was totally confused. I thought Blossom and Cackle were enemies, but now they were **SCREECHING** away like BFFs! What was next? Were they going to start dressing alike? Having sleepovers at each other's castles?

I stared at Blossom, trying to figure things out. She *seemed* like the same Blossom I had met on my first trip to the Kingdom of Fantasy.

She had on the same sparkly dress and shoes, and she had the same RiNg and earrings and rose crown. She also wore the same medallion with her name etched on the back.

At that moment, Blossom saw

rose crown

ring

earrings

medallion

some **black** roses in a vase. "Ah, black, my favorite color!" she whispered.

A **black rose** fell to the floor, and Blossom knelt to pick it up. As she bent down, her **medallion** flipped over.

It was then that I noticed something. The writing on the back of the medallion didn't say her name, **Blossom** of the Flowers.

It said another name . . .

WITHER OF THE FLOWERS

When I saw what it said, I understood immediately. This 𝒻𝒶𝒾𝓇𝓎 wasn't Blossom at all ... **it was her twin sister!**

Blossom

WITHER

I felt a huge **wave of relief** wash over me. So that's why Blossom had been so rude to me — because she wasn't really Blossom! She was Wither! And I was sure the real Blossom still considered me a GOOD FRIEND.

But where was the real Blossom now? I absolutely had to find out, and . . .

save her!

WE ARE CRUEL,
MAD, AND MEAN!

Right then I heard the *sound* of violin music spread through the air. It was a somber and unsettling tune . . .

Silver Violins

The silver violins are violins that have been bewitched. The dark fairies use them to play their musical spells, which fill those who can hear them with sadness.

The Secret Song of the Dark Fairies

We are dark fairies!
We are cruel, mad, and mean!
Our homeland is Mount Blast,
where there isn't any green.
The queen whom we serve
can sting like a thorn,
and if you ever cross her,
you'll wish you'd never
been born!

Which two dark fairies are identical?

Solution on page 579

Tons of dark fairies came into the room and danced around. Each fairy was playing a **silver violin** and singing the secret song of the dark fairies.

They mentioned **MOUNT BLAST** in their song. I remembered having read something about that **SPOOKY AREA** in *The Legendarium* . . .

MOUNT BLAST

Very little is known about Mount Blast, a region that lies beyond the borders of illusions and past the edges of dreams. The earth there is black because of the volcanic sand. The ground is boiling to the touch because the magma of a volcano flows beneath it. The air is always thick with smoke, and dark clouds that hang in the sky always block out the sun. The creatures that live there — the dark fairies — are extremely evil. They are devoted to Cackle, the queen of the witches.

BRING ME BLOSSOM!

Suddenly, Wither got up and *DISAPPEARED* behind a screen. A little while later, she reappeared. Instead of wearing her usual *fairy-blue* gown, she was dressed all in black.

"I, Wither, leader of the dark fairies, have an announcement to make!" she yelled. "I have taken Blossom's place, tricking everyone, even that no-good mouse!"

"WHAT A NO-GOOD MOUSE!"

the dark fairies echoed.

Wither went on to explain about the seven treasures. "I got that furbrain to bring them all

Before . . .

. . . and after!

to me. Now I can use them to **IMPRISON** my twin sister, Blossom, forever! Ugh! Her sappy, **sweet** personality is enough to give me a toothache!"

"A toothache!" the dark fairies repeated.

I rolled my eyes. The dark fairies sounded like a bunch of parakeets. Didn't they ever use their own brains?

Then the dark fairies called, "No one is smarter than you, O Wither!" And I realized I'd better figure out how Wither was going to imprison Blossom.

WITHER CLAPPED HER

HANDS AND ORDERED,

"BRING ME BLOSSOM!"

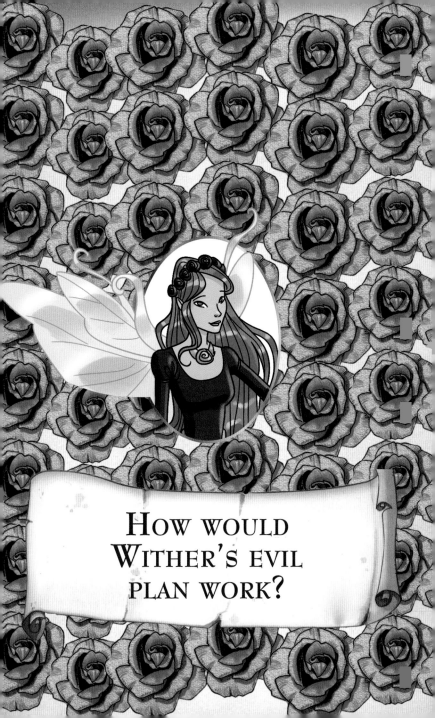

HOW WOULD WITHER'S EVIL PLAN WORK?

Seven hooded Knights of the Dark Tower brought out a stretcher with Blossom on it. She had the SWEET DREAMS CRADLE around her neck, and she was in a deep sleep.

"Thanks to the Sweet Dreams Cradle, the **first treasure** that the knight retrieved, Blossom will sleep forever! Ha, ha, ha! If Sir Geronimo of Stilton were here, I'm sure he'd be proud to see what his mission accomplished! Ha, ha, haaa!"

Oh, what had I done?

With the
FIRST TREASURE,
Blossom will sleep
forever!

Then Wither shrieked, "And now, bring me . . .

the second treasure: the Essence of Darkness!"

Nefaria brought her the BONE box that the Stinky Bats had given me. A dark cloud rose out of it as it opened.

"Hee, hee, heeee!" Wither cackled. "This will make Blossom's prison pitch-black . . .

DARKER THAN THE DARKEST NIGHT!"

With the
SECOND TREASURE,
her prison will
be pitch-black!

Next, Wither yelled for the **tHiRD treasure**. Four knights carried the CRYSTAL COFFIN into the room. They lifted up Blossom and put her inside.

Putrid Parmesan! This was getting way too **CREEPY**! Wither planned on locking her sister up inside the Crystal Coffin!

"This coffin will keep Blossom **IMPRISONED** for months . . . years . . . centuries! In other words, she'll never leave!"

All the dark fairies echoed her words, "Never leave . . ."

NEVER LEAVE NEVER LEAVE NEVER LEAVE
NEVER LEAVE NEVER LEAVE
NEVER LEAVE
NEVER LEAVE NEVER LEAVE
NEVER LEAVE
NEVER LEAVE NEVER LEAVE
NEVER LEAVE NEVER LEAVE
NEVER LEAVE

With the
THIRD TREASURE,
Blossom will be
locked up forever!

"What about the **fourth treasure**? What is that, Wither?" Cackle asked, excitedly.

Wither giggled. Talk about a **STRANGE** sense of humor! She held up the **GREEN** hair I had taken from the three Hairballs. Kneeling over the Crystal Coffin, she used the hair to tie Blossom's hands together.

"Now you will never ever be able to free yourself, Sister! And your kingdom will be **MINE** forever!"

She laughed wickedly.

And I felt so sad . . . so sad . . . so sad . . . so sad . . . so sad . . . so sad . . . so sad . . . so sad . . .

With the
FOURTH TREASURE,
Blossom will never be able
to free herself!

Nefaria handed Wither the **fifth treasure**: the vase of water containing the **STONE MASK**.

Wither turned toward the head Knight of the Dark Tower. "Bighead, who is more beautiful, she or I?" she asked.

Bighead coughed. The two fairies were **IDENTICAL**! "Well, um, you see . . ." the knight stammered.

The dark queen flew into a **rage**. She grabbed the mask and shoved it onto Blossom's face. "Now *I* am the most beautiful in the entire Kingdom of Fantasy! Me! Me! Me!"

All the Black Fairies repeated, "**ME! ME! ME!**"

"You fools! You mean, **'You! You! You!'**" Wither corrected them.

With the
FIFTH TREASURE,
her beauty will be hidden!

After that, Wither picked up the **sixth treasure**, the magical

CLICK-CLACK CHAIN.

"Careful, my queen. The chain is very dangerous," Bighead warned.

Wither shot him a **LOOK**. "Fool, do you think I was born yesterday? Of course I know it's dangerous!"

She lifted the chain, placed it around the Crystal Coffin, and said the magic words. The chain locked with a CLICK and a CLACK!

With the
SIXTH TREASURE,
Blossom will be
imprisoned
forever!

Finally, Wither took out the **seVenth tReasuRe**: the Condensed Sadness.

She grabbed the vial and poured the tears onto the coffin. They crystallized and formed a solid layer over the coffin.

With the crystal tears you couldn't see anyone was even in the coffin!

"Now you will be hidden — completely covered in sadness!" Wither yelled.

"SWEET DREAMS, SIS!"

CONDESNED SADNESS

With the
SEVENTH TREASURE,
Blossom will be
forgotten forever!

SMELLS LIKE MOUSE!

ither hid the coffin in a place that was very difficult to find because no one could see it:

THE INVISIBLE CRYPT!

See you soon, Cackle!

See you soon, Wither!

"Okay, show's over! Everyone get out!" Wither yelled at the dark fairies. "And if I catch anyone spying, I'll turn you into a warty toad!"

"Well done, my dear. Keep up that strictness! Let them know who is in charge!" Cackle praised her. "Now I'm off for the **KINGDOM OF WITCHES**!"

Wither went to the window to say good-bye to Cackle. Suddenly, she sniffed the air. "Smells like white roses," she said.

The scent of white roses?

"My queen, the scent comes from Blossom's beloved WHITE ROSE LABYRINTH," Bighead explained to her.

459

"Destroy it at once!" she shouted furiously. She sniffed again. "I also smell **MOUSE**!" she shrieked.

I turned PALE. Of course it smelled like mouse! Wither was smelling me!

I took a step backward and escaped down the dark hallway. I ran **here** and there and UP

I must escape!

and **down** and *right* and **LEFT** until I saw a door that opened onto the garden.

I ran outside as fast as I could, and then went through a GOLDEN GATE in the shape of a heart. It led me right to the White Rose Labyrinth!

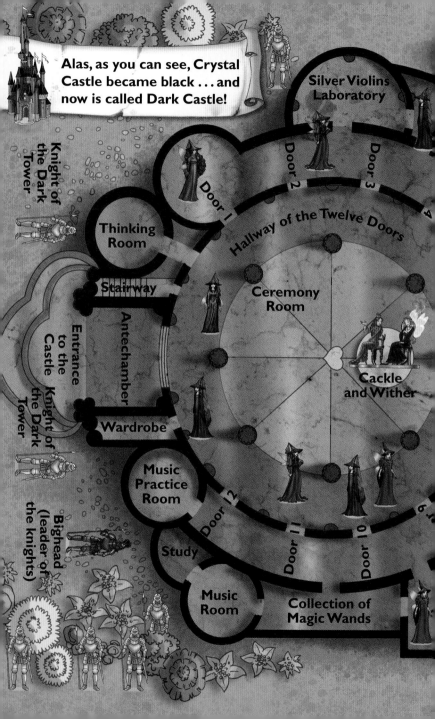

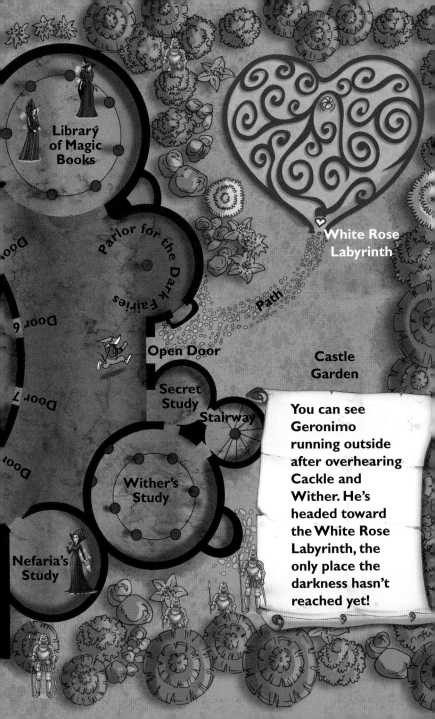

Library of Magic Books

Parlor for the Dark Fairies

Door 6

Door 7

Door

Open Door

Secret Study

Stairway

Wither's Study

Nefaria's Study

White Rose Labyrinth

Path

Castle Garden

You can see Geronimo running outside after overhearing Cackle and Wither. He's headed toward the **White Rose Labyrinth**, the only place the darkness hasn't reached yet!

THE WHITE ROSE
LABYRINTH

The White Rose Labyrinth was a small garden shaped like a **HEART**. It was made up of white *rosebushes* that formed a very TALL hedge.

The White Rose Labyrinth

White roses planted by Blossom grow here. They have a scent that is one thousand times stronger than normal roses, and they have no thorns! At the center of the labyrinth is the Fountain of Desires, which is protected by a mysterious wizard.

At the entrance of that scented flower maze was a tablet with a mysterious message engraved on it . . .

IN THE WHITE ROSE
LABYRINTH,

SPEAK FROM THE HEART

AND THE FOUNTAIN
OF DESIRES

WILL DO ITS PART.

JUST TELL THE WIZARD
WHAT YOU DESIRE,

STAND BACK, AND SEE
WHAT WILL TRANSPIRE!

Solution on page 579

Geronimo
has lost his
green gnome hat.
Where is it?

I ran between the rose hedges, making so many turns I felt **dizzy**! But just when I thought I was completely lost, I arrived at the heart of the labyrinth. I saw a small **WHITE** marble temple, which held a fountain.

Its base was a shell-shaped tub, with a **mysterious** statue standing over it. The statue depicted a hooded wizard. At his feet, I saw an engraved message in Fantasian:

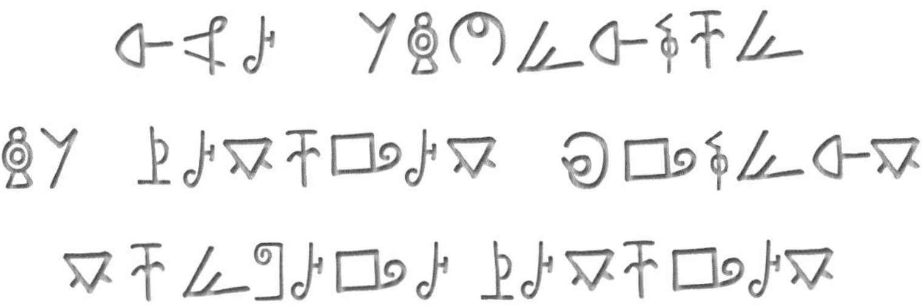

To translate the message yourself, you can find the Fantasian Alphabet on page 575. Or you can find the message in English on page 579.

I Wish . . .

I leaned over the tub with my head in my paws. I knew I had to **SAVE** Blossom. But how could I do it alone? I thought of all the friends that I had met during my voyages to the **Kingdom of Fantasy**. Maybe they could help me. It was worth a shot!

Peering into the **crystal waters**, I yelled, "I wish with all my *heart* that my friends were here: Thunderhorn and his sister, Emerald; and Princess Sterling with her dragon, Sparkle; and Blue Rider and Tenderheart; and Prince George; and Captain Coldheart; and King Skywings; and Oscar Roach;

Emerald

Captain Coldheart

King Skywings

and the ladybug queen, Bitsy Luckybug! And all my other friends, too!"

Bitsy Luckybug

Just thinking about my friends made me miss them. A **tear** fell down my cheek and fell into the fountain's tub: *drip!*

Oh, how I wish . . .

As soon as my tear hit the water, an **amazing** thing happened. The weird wizard statue came to life!

He said,

"I am the Wizard of Desires.

Your desire is sincere!

Your wish will be granted!"

He held his hands in the air, and a MIST rose from the fountain. Then, one by one, all my friends from the Kingdom of Fantasy came out of the fountain!

We're coming!
We are here to help you!
You can count on us!
We will save Blossom!
We are here for you, Knight!
Of course we'll help!
Bzzz!
Friends!
Don't worry!

Let's Form a Club!

ow! This was amazing! My wish had truly been granted. **I WASN'T ALONE ANYMORE! I WAS SO HAPPY!**

I hugged my dear friends one by one. I was a little embarrassed to be seen in a **gnome** disguise that was three sizes too **small**, but no one cared. I should have known. As my aunt Sweetfur always tells me, **true friends** don't care what you wear, they care about you!

Anyway, where was I? Oh, right. I thanked my friends for coming, then I said, "**We need to save Blossom!**"

I continued to explain. "Blossom has been imprisoned by her **EVIL** twin sister, Wither.

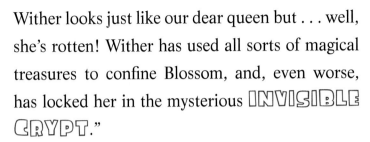

Wither looks just like our dear queen but . . . well, she's rotten! Wither has used all sorts of magical treasures to confine Blossom, and, even worse, has locked her in the mysterious INVISIBLE CRYPT."

George stepped forward. "That's terrible. Let's form a rescue committee!"

"Good idea," Oscar Roach agreed. "What should we call ourselves?"

Can you help me, friends?

George

Scribblehopper

Oscar Roach

Scribblehopper jumped up. "Since we are fighting to bring our queen back, how about we call ourselves **THE COME BACK CLUB**! And our symbol could be a **blue rose** the color of Blossom's eyes!" he croaked.

Everyone shouted, "Hooray for the Come Back Club!"

THE COME BACK CLUB

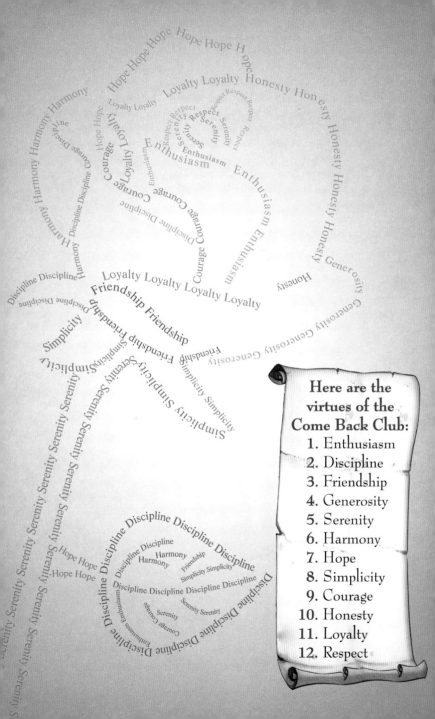

Here are the virtues of the **Come Back Club:**

1. Enthusiasm
2. Discipline
3. Friendship
4. Generosity
5. Serenity
6. Harmony
7. Hope
8. Simplicity
9. Courage
10. Honesty
11. Loyalty
12. Respect

1. Sparkle
2. Dragon of Time
3. Unicorn of Dreams
4. Scribblehopper
5. Thunderhorn
6. Princess Sterling
7. Tyler Terrain and Eartha
8. Boils
9. Beatrice Bigfoot
10. Strongheart
11. Vol
12. Tenderheart
13. Blue Rider
14. George
15. Honor
16. Cozy
17. Factual
18. Snowy Dawn
19. Blizzard

THE COME BACK CLUB

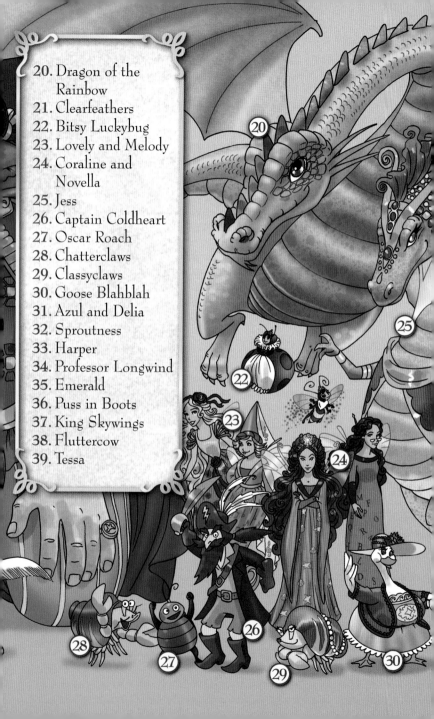

As we made our rescue plans, the Wizard of Desires urged us on. "Look for a *heart-shaped silver plate* that hides a secret passageway . . ."

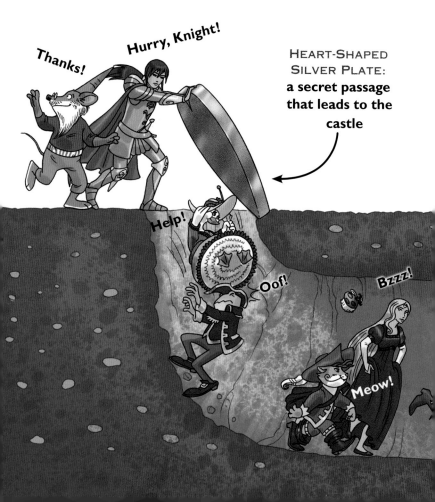

HEART-SHAPED SILVER PLATE: **a secret passage that leads to the castle**

Thanks!

Hurry, Knight!

Help!

Oof!

Bzzz!

Meow!

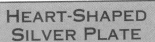

A group of us raced for the **SILVER PLATE**. The wizard had explained that the secret passageway would lead us right to the Ceremony Room.

When we found the plate, **Blue Rider** lifted it up, and we all scrambled inside.

TELL THE KNIGHT!

It was dark in the passageway. Chatterclaws rummaged through his shell and found a **CANDLE**. "It's a good thing I've got the **Chatterhouse** with all my whatchamacallits," he said. "Otherwise, we wouldn't be able to see a thing! Seriously, I couldn't . . ."

While he **chattered** on, we all gathered around the candlelight. I opened *The Legendarium* to see what I could find out about the mysterious **INVISIBLE CRYPT**.

THE
SECRET
OF THE
INVISIBLE
CRYPT

To understand the Invisible Crypt, you must first understand how Crystal Castle was built . . .

Crystal Castle was founded by King Regal III, the royal fairy father. He is the first forefather of the Winged Dynasty. The Winged Ones are the purest creatures of the Kingdom of Fantasy. A true Winged One is not capable of lying, and his heart is as pure as crystal. King Regal wanted to build a castle that was also pure and transparent. He asked Quartzy, the king of the Crystalline Gnomes and the most experienced crystal worker in the kingdom, to do the job.

King Regal III

CRYSTALLINE GNOMES

These gnomes lived in
Crystal County, beyond
the River of No Return, at
the edge of the Kingdom
of Fantasy. They mined
the purest crystal in the
kingdom. It reflected the light
of a thousand rays! It took three
hundred thirty thousand years to
build the castle. But in the end, it was the most
beautiful castle in the kingdom!

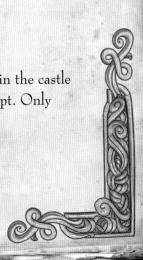

Quartzy

THE INVISIBLE CRYPT

The gnomes built a secret room in the castle
that they called the Invisible Crypt. Only
they know where it is!

I put down the book and scratched my head. "Hmm, so I guess only the Crystalline Gnomes know where to find the Invisible Crypt. But where can we find a **Crystalline Gnome**?!" I muttered.

Right then I noticed Cozy giving her husband, Factual, a **HARD** elbow. "Go ahead, Factual," she said. **"Tell the Knight!"**

Okay, okay!

Tell him now!

Factual,
King of the Gnomes

Cozy,
Queen of the Gnomes

Factual stepped forward. "Sir Geronimo, what I have to tell you is that my grandfather's grandfather's grandfather's grandfather's grandfather's grandfather's grandfather's grandfather's grandfather's grandfather's grandfather's grandfather's grandfather's grandfather's grandfather's grandfather's grandfather's grandfather's grandfather . . . was Quartzy, the king of the Crystalline Gnomes!"

Factual continued speaking, and his voice ECHOED through the tunnel. "Now I will tell you a secret. I know the **Riddle of the Invisible Crypt**! The solution to the riddle tells how to reach the crypt . . . but the riddle is **HARD** to answer — very hard. No one has ever been able to solve it. But maybe you can solve it!"

Then he lowered his voice and whispered, "Here is the mysterious riddle . . ."

mysterious riddle
mysterious riddle
e mysterious riddle
e mysterious riddle
the mysterious riddle
is the mysterious riddle
ere is the mysterious riddle
Here is the mysterious riddle...

THE RIDDLE OF
THE INVISIBLE CRYPT

To reach the crypt, you must find
a place that reflects you and your mind.
This place makes portraits at all hours;
it's made with magical crystal powers.
So take a step and look around.
It might be up, or it might be down!

I thought and thought, but I was still confused. What did that riddle mean? We headed farther along underground until we found another heart-shaped silver plate. I lifted it up a tiny bit and peered out. We had made it to the Ceremony Room! But the dark fairies and the **KNIGHTS OF THE DARK TOWER** were everywhere. Gulp!

Gulp!

HEY, DARK FAIRIES!

I studied the Ceremony Room. We needed to find the **MYSTERIOUS** crypt, but how would we do it with all those dark fairies and knights around?

Suddenly, something **shook** the castle.

It was Strongheart the giant — a member of the Come Back Club! He was shaking the tower of the **castle** with his big strong hands! Next to him, Beatrice Bigfoot ripped the whole roof **OFF** the castle.

Ah, it was nice to have strong friends!

The **DRAGON OF THE RAINBOW** blew flames into the castle, roaring, "Hey, dark fairies, how would you like to play with fire?!"

The fairies all began yelling at once. "Get lost, Fireface!"

"We'll make DRAGON HOT DOGS out of you!"

Dragon Hot Dogs

"Or maybe **dragon soup**!"

"Oh, please!" the dragon countered. "You tiny fairies couldn't touch me with a ten-foot pole!"

I was beginning to think maybe this battle would be easier than I thought. I mean, in comparison to the dark fairies, my friends were **huge**! Unfortunately, before I could start celebrating our success, I heard a **shriek** that froze my blood.

Dragon Soup

It was Wither, and she was shouting furiously.

"How dare you challenge me and my court! Foulbreath, prepare for **battle**!"

Foulbreath?

A minute later, a black dragon with terribly **stinky** fire breath arrived. "Your wish is my command, my queen!" she hissed.

I should have known. Who else would have a dragon named Foulbreath? The dragon had flaming scales, **RED** eyes, steel claws, and a helmet with a **LARGE** ruby.

Foulbreath approached the window of the castle, and Wither **jumped** on her back. "Dragon of the Rainbow, I will be back!

Attack! Attack! Attack!
Attack! Attack! Attack!
Attack! Attack! Attack!
Attack! Attack! Attack!
Attack! Attack! Attack!

And you will pay for your **rudeness**!" the dark fairy shrieked.

The dragon flew away, and the entire

Your wish is my command!

court of dark fairies and the knights of the Dark Tower fled behind them. Thank goodness they were gone. That dragon's FOUL BREATH was enough to make me gag!

I turned to the **DRAGON OF THE RAINBOW**. "Thanks for your courage," I told my friend.

Solution on page 579

HMM . . . HMM . . . HMM . . .

rystal Castle was finally deserted! We began to search and search through it . . . but couldn't find the **INVISIBLE CRYPT**.

I thought and thought and thought. In order to find the **crypt**, we first had to solve the RIDDLE. What can paint portraits at all hours? What can reflect you and your mind? What is made up of magical powers?

To reach the crypt, you must find a place that reflects you and your mind. This place makes portraits at all hours; it's made with magical crystal powers. So take a step and look around. It might be up, or it might be down!

Hmm . . . hmm . . . hmm . . .

At that moment, I noticed a heavy velvet curtain in the corner. It was covering a *mysterious object*. When I moved the curtain, I saw myself reflected in a mirror.

"That's it!" I squeaked. "A mirror makes **portraits** at all hours!"

Hmm?

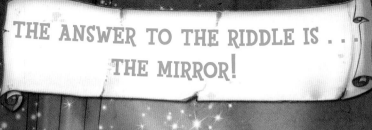

THE ANSWER TO THE RIDDLE IS . . .
THE MIRROR!

There was writing ENGRAVED at the bottom of the mirror. I bent to take a closer look, then read the words aloud:

"I, Quartzy, the king of the Crystalline Gnomes, created the mysterious Invisible Crypt. This magical mirror will take you there!"

I brought my paw up to the mirror . . .

My paw went through the mirror, and I could see a staircase.

I put my paw on the mirror. It went **through** the surface! Then I stuck my foot in. It went through, too! And I could see a 𝖘𝖙𝖆𝖎𝖗𝖈𝖆𝖘𝖊 in front of me.

"Come on!" I called to my friends. "I found the entrance to the **Invisible Crypt**!"

Then I stuck my foot in . . . and it went through the mirror, too!

Magic Mirrors
In the Kingdom of Fantasy, there are many magic mirrors. Each one hides a secret. This mirror leads to a crystal staircase, which leads down to the mysterious Invisible Crypt!

GOOD LUCK!

Instead of following me into the mirror, Scribblehopper handed me a torch. "Since you are the most **COURAGEOUS**, Sir Knight, we decided the HONOR of entering the INVISIBLE CRYPT should be all yours! Good luck!"

I turned pale. Oh, why didn't my friends see that I really wasn't courageous at all! I was scared of a million things, like **SPIDERS**, the dark, and that spooky sci-fi ringtone on my cell phone. Still, I didn't want to disappoint everyone, so . . .

I gathered all my courage . . .
crossed through the magic mirror . . .
and descended down, down, down . . .

 510

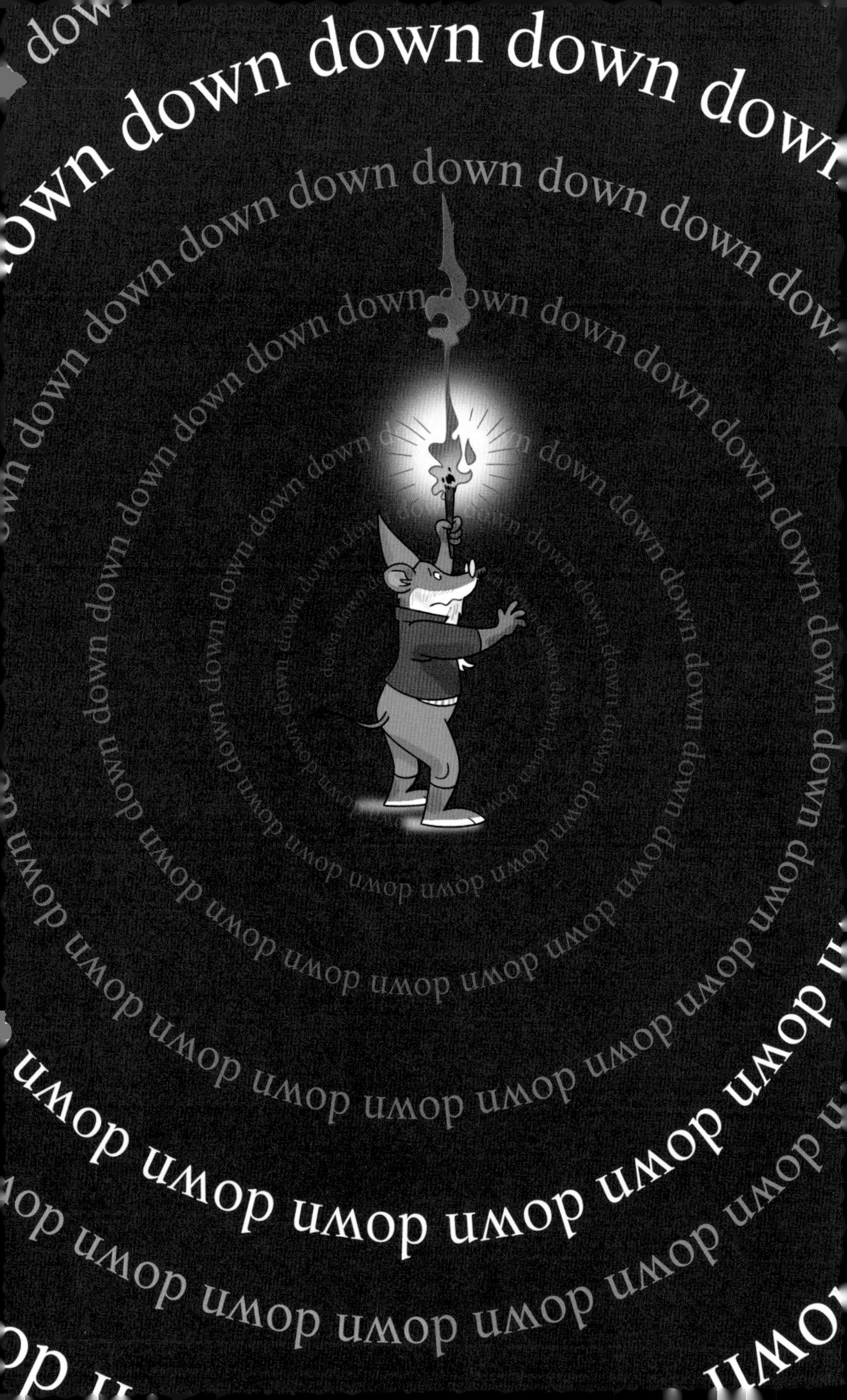
down down down down down

Finally, I reached the bottom of the staircase. At the end, I found the Invisible Crypt!

It was completely dark because of the **Essence of Darkness** that Wither had **sprinkled** around the CRYSTAL COFFIN. *Okay, first things first*, I said to myself. *How can I* **cancel out** *the dark of the Essence of Darkness?*

As I racked my brain, I remembered the stardust I had received from Flyola.

I threw the bright stardust in the air . . . and the crypt LIT UP completely!

Stardust

HERE'S HOW I CANCELED OUT THE ESSENCE OF DARKNESS!

The coffin was covered in crystallized Condensed Sadness. To undo the spell, I knew I needed to find CONDENSED HAPPINESS.

So I thought about a happy memory. I remembered the first time that I met Blossom. Just thinking about her brought tears of **joy** to my eyes. My tears **fell** on the crystals, and they melted!

HERE'S HOW I GOT RID OF THE CONDENSED SADNESS!

Now I needed to cancel out the spell of the **CLICK-CLACK CHAIN**. This one was easier, since Redhot had told me the reverse magic words!

Carefully, I recited them:

"Click-clack, reverse back!
Untie, chain, piddlypack!"

With a metallic noise, the chain opened!

HERE'S HOW I UNTIED
THE CLICK-CLACK CHAIN!

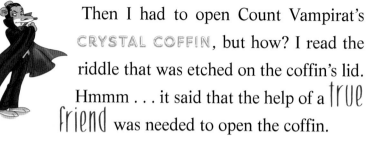

Then I had to open Count Vampirat's CRYSTAL COFFIN, but how? I read the riddle that was etched on the coffin's lid. Hmmm . . . it said that the help of a true friend was needed to open the coffin.

I scratched my head. A true friend? Hey, that was me! I was a **true friend** of Blossom! I lifted the lid right off (though it was extremely heavy)!

HERE'S HOW I OPENED THE CRYSTAL COFFIN!

Now that the coffin was open, I could hear the music of the SWEET DREAMS CRADLE. That song was DANGEROUS — it could put me to sleep forever! So I took off my shirt and wrapped it around my ears. Then I threw the cradle on the ground and stomped on it! **CRUNCH!**

HERE'S HOW I GOT RID OF THE SWEET DREAMS CRADLE!

 Once I got rid of the cradle, I had to remove the Hairballs' **green hair** that was tied around Blossom's hands.

I couldn't **cut** the hair, since I didn't have the Claw Clips. But I could untie the knots! So I did!

HERE'S HOW I UNTIED THE HAIRBALLS' GREEN HAIR!

Finally, I had to remove the **STONE MASK**.

To protect myself from the danger of such an evil object, I thought **good thoughts**, then I lifted the mask off Blossom and quickly slipped it back into the vase of **water**. Whew, I had done it!

HERE'S HOW I PUT THE STONE MASK BACK IN ITS PLACE!

For a moment, nothing happened. I stared at my friend lying in the CRYSTAL COFFIN. This was the moment of truth! Would she **WAKE UP**? Would she recognize me? And if she did, would she wonder why I was dressed in such a strange, tight-fitting gnome outfit? I couldn't wait to get back into my real clothes. Those gnome pants were so tight I could hardly breathe!

I was still thinking about my gnome disguise when **Blossom** opened her eyes. "I knew you would come for me, fearless knight!" she said.

I grinned. And right then I **smelled** a sweet, delicate aroma.

It was the mythical Scent of Fantasy!

I CHALLENGE YOU!

I helped Blossom out of the Crystal Coffin. We walked up the stairs together, crossed through the **mirror**, and found ourselves in the Ceremony Room.

The Come Back Club was so excited. "Hooray!" everyone shouted. "Our beloved queen has returned!"

Unfortunately, our *happiness* didn't last long. Wither had also returned to the castle. She shrieked at Blossom,

"I CHALLENGE YOU TO A MAGIC FAIRY DUEL. WHOEVER WINS WILL RULE OVER THE KINGDOM OF FANTASY!"

Blossom was up to the task.

"I accept your challenge!"

Magic Fairy Duel!

Foulbreath the Dark Dragoness

Color of scales: black
Eye color: red
Breath: stinks of ashes
Voice: shrill
Harness: red silk, adorned with rubies
Powers: stinky fire breath, a voice that deafens because of its evilness, and lightning speed.

Foulbreath is skilled in acrobatics and studied at the Witchdragon Flight Academy of Dark Mountain. She is a descendant of the noble line of Terrifying Dragons.

JESS THE JEWELED DRAGONESS

Color of scales: pure white
Eye color: blue
Breath: candy-scented
Voice: very sweet
Harness: golden, adorned with precious stones
Powers: purifying fire breath, a voice that charms with its sweetness, and lightning speed.

Jess is skilled in acrobatics and studied at the Fairydragon Flight Academy of Light Mountain. She descends from the noble line of Silver Dragons.

Wither attacked first.

She let out a WILD SHRIEK, and
a purple flash of light shot from her magic
wand. Blossom ducked and counterattacked
by waving her own wand and letting out a blue
flash of light.

Then Wither threw a flurry of FIREBALLS!
Yikes!

I will win!

May the best fairy win!

Blossom defended herself with a clear and powerful LIGHT SHIELD.

She called all the butterflies of the Kingdom of Fantasy to protect her. So Wither called all the BATS.

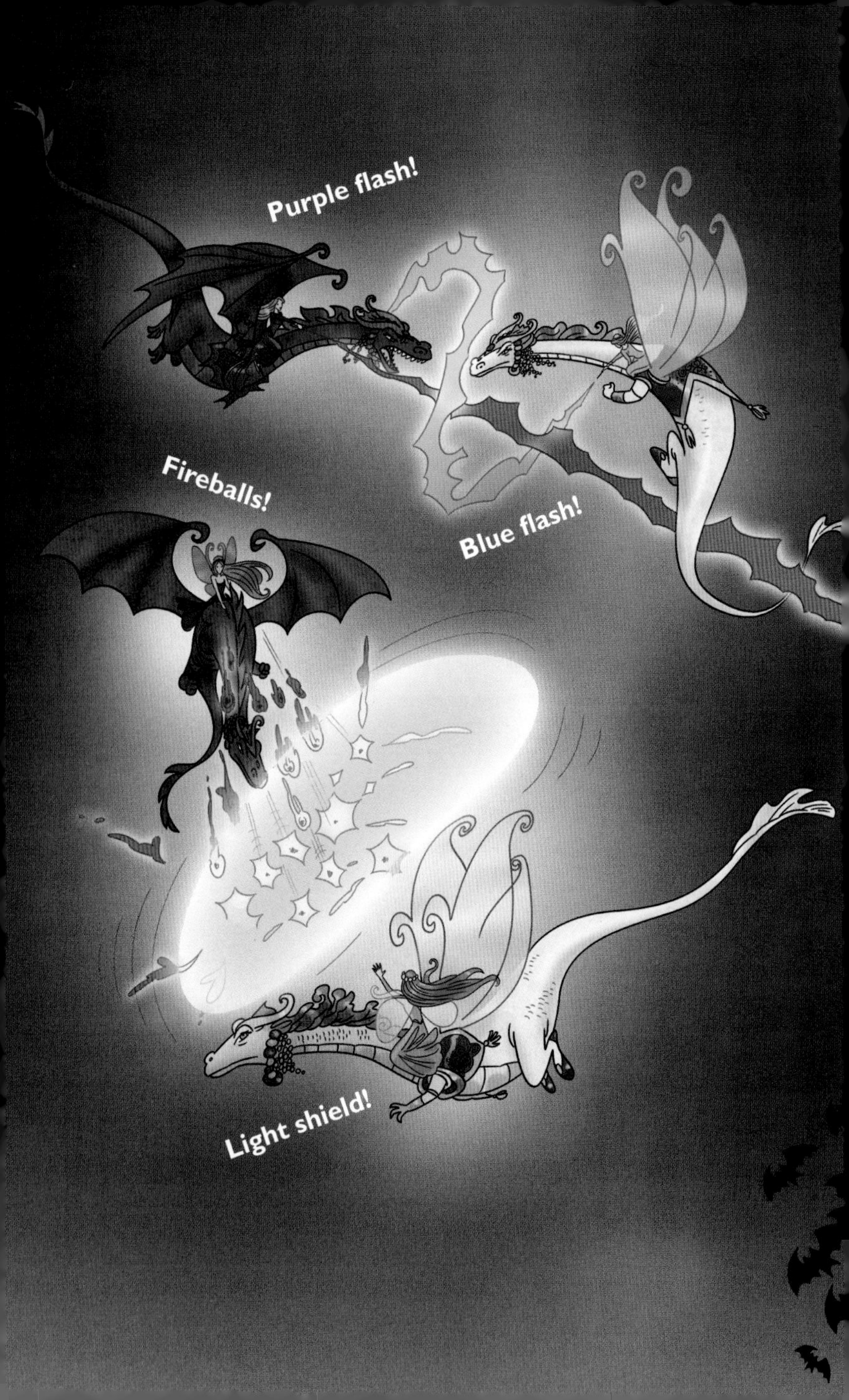
Purple flash!
Blue flash!
Fireballs!
Light shield!

I challenge you with my butterflies!
I challenge you with my bats!

Wow! What a duel!
Two powerful sisters
challenging each other while
riding their prized dragons.

The magic of good . . .
and the magic of evil!

Wither soared higher in the sky and then nose-dived toward her sister. But **Blossom** created a giant net of moon rays. Wither *bounced* off the moon rays and began to fall at an alarming rate.

"Aaaaahhhhh! The old net trick!" she shrieked.

BZZZT! BUUURP! PFFFF!

Wither plunged through the air in a swirl of black. Was this the end? Would she end up in one **withered** heap?

Not this time. Right before she hit the ground, Cackle, queen of the witches, flew to her rescue. She was riding the most incredible stinky flying monster. The creature scooped up Wither in a net, then flew away as quick as LIGHTNING!

The whole crowd gasped,

"WHOOOOOOOOOOOOOOOOOOOOOOOOOOOOOOOOAAAAAAAAAAAA!"

What was that flying beast with BAT wings and a boar's face? I leafed frantically through *The Legendarium* and found out that it was a STINKYPUS.

Back to the Kingdom of the Witches!

With stinky pleasure!

As the stinkypus flew away, he shot out an extremely powerful flame. **BZZZZT**!

Then he let out a very noisy burp. **BUUURP!**

Finally, he gave out a terribly stinky fart. **Pffffffff!**

The stench was so strong, even the flowers wilted!

"We'll be back!" Cackle warned as she **FLEW** off.

Wither added something from the **NET**, but all we could make out was "We will mffffg mfffg mfffg!"

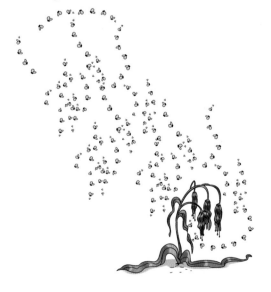

STINKYPUS

Bzzzzt!

The stinkypus is one of Cackle's flying mounted beasts. He is very large and has stinky breath, porcupine quills, bat wings, and a boar's head. He can devour anything but has a hard time digesting most things. As a result, he burps loudly and farts a lot! He is so stinky, he's always surrounded by a cloud of gnats!

Fur color: sewer-colored

Eye color: sewer-colored

Breath: stinks of sewage

Cry: sounds like the gurgle of a sewer when it rains

Habits: He never takes baths, and he brushes his teeth with (you guessed it) sewer water!

Her threats were lost in the wind as they flew—and so was the stench of the stinkypus. Thank goodmouse!

We will mfffg!

The Magic Fairy Duel was over, and our beloved Blossom had won!

Everyone crowded around the queen. We were so relieved that the kindhearted sister had won the battle.

I looked around at all the SMILING faces. That's when I noticed that the Dragon of the Rainbow was grinning from ear to ear. But he wasn't looking at the queen. He was staring at Jess the Jeweled Dragoness, and he had a goofy, **dreamy** expression.

"Isn't she wonderful?" he said to me, pointing at Jess. "She's so KIND and caring and cute. I've liked her for years and years. But I'm too SHY to tell her."

So I decided to introduce them.

The two dragons hit it off *IMMEDIATELY*. They went off together, talking about flying and **FLAMES** and all sorts of dragon things. It turns out I'm not only a mouse, I'm a matchmaker! Who knew?

LOVE! DRAGON LOVE! DRAGON

AND BLOSSOM SPOKE

lossom stepped out onto the balcony of Crystal Castle and addressed everyone.

"My beloved subjects, **LIGHT** has won against **DARKNESS**. The time has now come to restore harmony to Crystal Castle!"

She lightly touched the black castle with her magic wand. The building began to shimmer and sparkle. Before long, the entire castle had returned to its **BRIGHT** and shiny CRYSTAL state! Everyone cheered.

"My subjects, I am so sorry my twin sister, **Wither**, treated you all so horribly. We may look alike, but we are very different. We both belong to the Winged Dynasty, but alas, her

 540

Blossom and Geronimo

heart is dark and **frozen** like a winter's night.

"I would never close the castle doors to you. And I would never humiliate my friend Sir Geronimo.

"It was all the doing of my evil twin sister, Wither!"

"And now, let me tell you the story of the Winged Ones . . ."

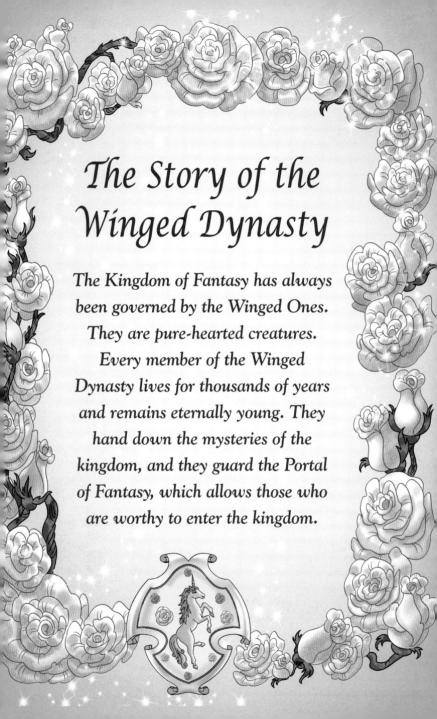

The Story of the Winged Dynasty

The Kingdom of Fantasy has always been governed by the Winged Ones. They are pure-hearted creatures. Every member of the Winged Dynasty lives for thousands of years and remains eternally young. They hand down the mysteries of the kingdom, and they guard the Portal of Fantasy, which allows those who are worthy to enter the kingdom.

The Story of Blossom and Wither

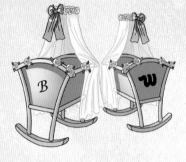

One day long ago, twin sisters named Blossom and Wither were born.

Each one received a silver fairy medallion with her name engraved on it.

Scarlet Skull Butterfly

But Wither was stung by a poisonous butterfly sent by Cackle. Her heart turned evil.

I want to become a witch!

Teach me to be evil!

I shall!

Wither fled Crystal Castle. She went to the Kingdom of the Witches and asked Cackle to teach her how to be a witch. Cackle did, and alas, Wither became an expert. Finally, she returned to Crystal Castle to steal the throne from Blossom.

The fake Blossom: actually Wither!

PRINCE FEARLESS!

After Blossom finished her story, she turned to me and **Smiled**. "Once more, dear knight, you have saved me and the entire Kingdom of Fantasy," she said. "For that, I would like to give you this reward!"

She waved her magic wand and sang:

"You deserve an honor

like never before.

I will make you a prince

for now and ever more!"

A **flash of light** surrounded me as Blossom announced, "From now on, you will be called . . .

Fearless, the Prince of the Winged Ones!"

Then she led me over to a mirror. I now had a blue complexion, and two wings sprouted from my back! I wore a *crown* on my head. Wow! I really looked like a **prince**!

Blossom gave me a sword. Its name was **BRAVE ONE**.

Brave One
This mythical sword is made of sparkling fairy crystal. It has a silver handle engraved with three roses, and a very sharp blade.

Now you are a Winged One!

Oooooh!

Blossom led me to the balcony. When I looked down, I saw all my friends. "Thank you for making me a prince, Blossom," I told the queen. "But I couldn't have done this alone."

Blossom smiled. "Don't worry, **PRINCE FEARLESS**," she assured me. "I have many more rewards!"

Then she gave each member of the Come Back Club a gift.

What an honor!

Don't worry, Prince. I have more rewards!

A red jacket for Scribblehopper!

Replenished treasure for the fireflies!

A diamond for Spitfire!

New silver armor for a real knight!

A spare shell for Chatterclaws!

Raspberry juice for the gnomes!

Blossom's Gifts

A Dragon Wedding

inally, **PEACE**, **happiness**, and **LOVE** had returned to the Kingdom of Fantasy! Everything was as it should be.

And, speaking of love, just then the Dragon of the Rainbow spoke up with an announcement. "Jess and I are getting MARRIED!" How wonderful! Preparations began immediately.

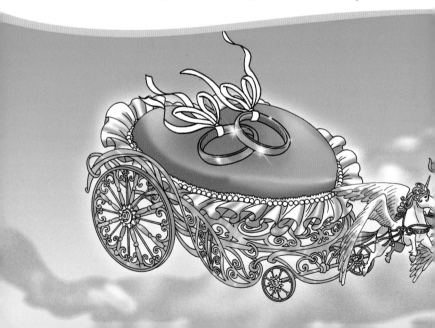

The next day, a carriage pulled by seven white **UNICORNS** flew up to Crystal Castle. The carriage held a blue pillow with two giant golden *wedding rings* resting on it.

Everyone in the kingdom had been invited to the dragon wedding. Even the **Phoenix of Destiny** arrived and offered to take me for a ride around Enchanted City.

Dragon Wedding Rings

"Your **wish** is my command, Prince!" The phoenix laughed as I climbed onto her back.

"I'll be back in time for the wedding!" I told everyone. Then we took off into the **beautiful** sunset.

I could hear the crowd beneath me cheering. "Hooray for Prince Fearless!" I felt like a real celebrity.

The Dragon of the Rainbow
and
Jess the Jeweled Dragoness
invite you to their wedding, today,
at Crystal Castle in the Ceremony Room.

Can you find the
seven phoenix feathers
hidden throughout
the book?

As we flew, the phoenix told
me a secret. "Since I saw you last,
I have lost **seven fire
feathers**. Who knows
where they went?"

Solution on page 580

Eventually, the phoenix brought me back to Crystal Castle, and I met up with all my **friends**. As I walked through the hallways of the castle, I heard someone calling, "Kniiiiight! I mean, Prinnnnnnce!"

I recognized the voice immediately. It was *Scribblehopper*, my literary frog friend!

"Um, so, I was wondering . . . if you don't need it anymore, can I have *The Legendarium* back?" he croaked.

I was so embarrassed. But I had to tell my friend the truth — about the dragon and the **fireball** and what happened to the book. "Well, you see, um, there was a little accident," I began.

Luckily, Scribblehopper took it all in stride. "It's okay, Prince. Actually, I have a lot of

My poor book! Burned to a crisp!

I will write another one . . .

I have tons of froggy ideas!

ideas for another book! I was thinking maybe I could write about . . ."

Scribblehopper croaked on and on, and **WEDDING BELLS** began to chime. The great dragon wedding had begun! Everything was **ENORMOUSE**, especially the

 *wedding cake*!

ONE MORE GIFT

As the wedding celebration continued, **Blossom** pulled me aside. "Tomorrow you will return home, Prince Geronimo. But before you go, I have one more gift for you," she said.

From a crystal JEWELRY BOX lined with blue silk, the queen removed a **silver** fairy ring with a sparkling sapphire in it. "Prince, you are a Winged One now," she said as she handed me the ring. "This ring, with the emblem of the Winged Dynasty on it, will allow you to cross through the Portal of Fantasy and leave the kingdom. The ring will also allow you to return whenever you want! But be warned. Take **special** care of the ring. It could be very

The Winged Ring

This enchanted ring is made of fairy
silver. It holds a sparkling blue sapphire
and the rose emblem. It can only
be worn by those who belong to the
Winged Dynasty. Whoever holds this
ring has the power to travel to and
from all the Lands of Fantasy.

dangerous if it fell into the wrong hands."

I thanked Blossom and took the ring. Then I realized I had **NO IDEA** how to use it!

But the queen explained that I simply had to **RUB** the ring and say these magic words:

"Winged ring, with your magical lore, please open the Portal of Fantasy door!"

"Are you ready to leave?" Blossom asked.

I nodded. Don't get me wrong, I love all my friends in the Kingdom of Fantasy, but I was really starting to miss my friends and family back home.

Waving good-bye, I **RUBBED** the ring and recited the magic words.

Immediately, a blue vortex opened in front of me, sucking me in. I heard **Blossom's** voice in the distance. "Good-bye, Geronimo! See you soon!"

The blue vortex transformed into all the colors of the rainbow. I was crossing through the Portal of Fantasy!

I was going HOME!

I'm going home!

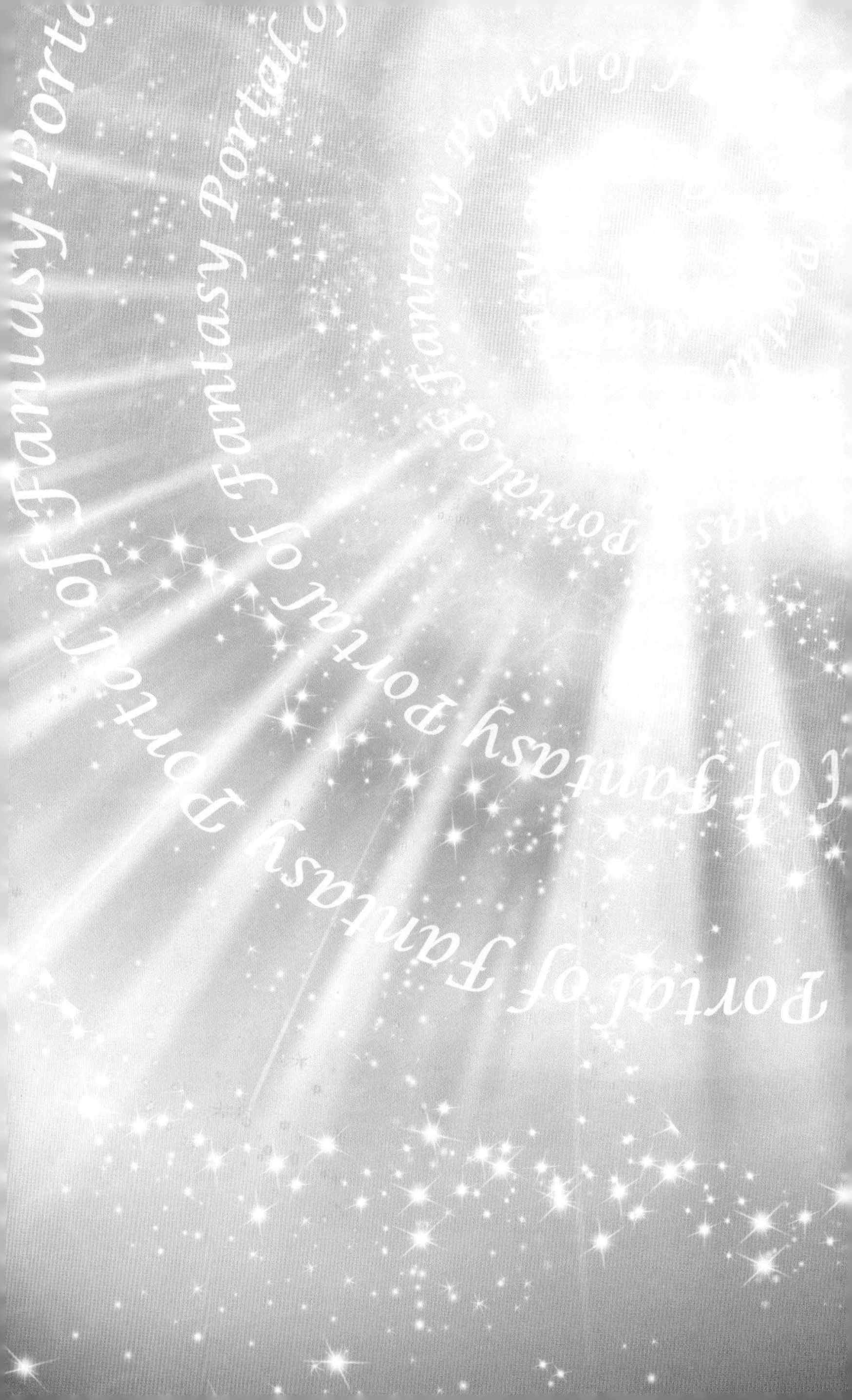

I Have an Epic Idea!

uddenly, I was back at my house in New Mouse City. I was sitting in my favorite **PAWCHAIR**, in front of my fireplace, watching the last **EMBERS** of the fire die out.

I stretched and yawned. Holey cheese! What had just happened? Then it all started coming back to me. The Phoenix of Destiny, Crystal Castle, Wither, the dragon wedding . . .

I sighed dreamily. Ah, what a wonderful adventure in the Kingdom of Fantasy! And this time I wasn't just a knight — I had become Prince Fearless of the Winged Dynasty!

But was it just a dream? I looked over at the table next to my chair — and there was the ring with the shining sapphire. It was real!

With that ring, I had become a Winged One. I could return to the Kingdom of Fantasy anytime I wanted. All I had to do was say the magic words for the portal to open. What were they? Oh yes.

"Winged ring with your magical lore, open the — "

I **CLAMPED** my paw to my mouth. I wasn't really ready for another adventure in the Kingdom of Fantasy just yet! After all, it felt like I had been away from home for forever. I had places to go. Rodents to see. **Chocolaty chocolate chip cookies** to eat.

Here is the Portal of Fantasy!

I was just taking a nibble on one of my cookies when the telephone rang.

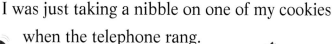

RING, RINNNNNNG!

I picked it up right away. "What took you so LONG, Grandson? I don't have all day!" my grandfather William's voice shouted. "Did you come up with an idea for the **epic adventure**? Did you start writing yet?"

I smiled under my whiskers. "Yes, Grandfather, I do have an idea," I squeaked. "I mean, I have an EPIC idea to write about an **epic** trip to the Kingdom of Fantasy. I think it will be exactly what you're looking for."

My grandfather **thundered**, "So what are you waiting for? Less thinking, more working!"

Then he hung up.

I put another log onto the fire. Staring at the **FLAMES**, I thought about the fiery red phoenix. I could have used one of the bird's magical feathers as my pen to write this extra-special story. But it was okay. After all, the bird's job wasn't to give me a **magical** pen, it was to deliver me to the Kingdom of Fantasy and to my **destiny**. After all, now I could return there again and again!

I had lost my fountain **pen** and **notebook** on my adventure, so I **tapped** away on my laptop. The memories of my travels were so clear.

I **wrote** and **wrote** and **wrote**.

When I was finished, I

Search throughout the book to find where Geronimo's notebook and fountain pen are hiding!

Solution on page 580

571

put the blue ring into the pocket of my jacket, close to my **HEART**. It would remind me of **Blossom** and all my friends in the Kingdom of Fantasy. And I would be ready at a moment's notice to go there and lend a helping paw!

So, dear readers, I won't say good-bye . . . I'll say "**SEE YOU SOON!**"

I know I will have many more adventures in the Kingdom of Fantasy. It is my DESTINY! And as a faithful author and friend, I will make sure to always tell you all about them.

A mouse hug and a cheesy good-bye from your affectionate mouse friend,

Geronimo Stilton

The End

Fantasian Alphabet

A   B   C   D   E

F   G   H   I   J

K   L   M   N   O

P   Q   R   S   T

U   V   W   X   Y   Z

0   1   2   3   4   5   6   7   8   9

Page 30
Dragon Landing

Pages 80–81
There are eight ships in bottles.

Pages 114–115

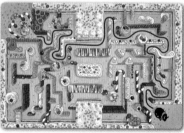

Pages 180–181
The gorilla costume is hidden on the bottom right, behind the wardrobe.

Pages 74–75
There are twenty-one bats.

Page 107

Pages 152–153

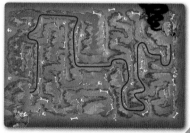

SOLUTIONS

Pages 204–205

Pages 216–217

Pages 220–221
There are fourteen pairs of eyes.

Pages 268–269

Page 287
There are seventeen bones.

Pages 270–271
There are twelve snails.

SOLUTIONS

Pages 292–293
There are twelve Little
Leaf Fairies. ————————→

Page 299
The Stone Mask

Pages 316–317

Pages 318–319
There are forty-eight fish.

Page 335
The Click-Clack Chain

Pages 360–361

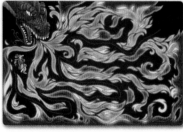

Page 365
"I want to die of old age!"

Pages 366–367
There are twenty gnomes.

Page 368
The dragon has four
legs, even if it seems
like he has more!

Page 369
You can see both: a cup
in the lighter part and
two faces in the darker
part.

SOLUTIONS

Pages 394–395

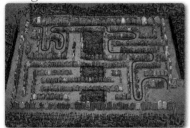

Pages 434–435

Pages 466–467

Page 469
The Fountain of Desires grants sincere desires.

Pages 502–503

SOLUTIONS

Page 555
The Seven Fire Feathers can be found on:

Page 77

Page 123

Page 142

Page 294

Page 311

Page 404

Page 498

Page 571
Geronimo's notebook and pen are hidden on page 63.

ABOUT THE AUTHOR

 Born in New Mouse City, Mouse Island, **GERONIMO STILTON** is Rattus Emeritus of Mousomorphic Literature and of Neo-Ratonic Comparative Philosophy. For the past twenty years, he has been running *The Rodent's Gazette*, New Mouse City's most widely read daily newspaper.

Stilton was awarded the Ratitzer Prize for his scoops on *The Curse of the Cheese Pyramid* and *The Search for Sunken Treasure*. He has also received the Andersen 2000 Prize for Personality of the Year. One of his bestsellers won the 2002 eBook Award for world's best ratlings' electronic book. His works have been published all over the globe.

In his spare time, Mr. Stilton collects antique cheese rinds and plays golf. But what he most enjoys is telling stories to his nephew Benjamin.

Be sure to read all of our magical special edition adventures!

THE KINGDOM OF FANTASY

THE QUEST FOR PARADISE:
THE RETURN TO THE KINGDOM OF FANTASY

THE AMAZING VOYAGE:
THE THIRD ADVENTURE IN THE KINGDOM OF FANTASY

THE DRAGON PROPHECY:
THE FOURTH ADVENTURE IN THE KINGDOM OF FANTASY

THE VOLCANO OF FIRE:
THE FIFTH ADVENTURE IN THE KINGDOM OF FANTASY

THE SEARCH FOR TREASURE:
THE SIXTH ADVENTURE IN THE KINGDOM OF FANTASY

THE ENCHANTED CHARMS
THE SEVENTH ADVENTURE IN THE KINGDOM OF FANTASY

THE PHOENIX OF DESTINY:
AN EPIC KINGDOM OF FANTASY ADVENTURE

THEA STILTON: THE JOURNEY TO ATLANTIS

THEA STILTON: THE SECRET OF THE FAIRIES

THEA STILTON: THE SECRET OF THE SNOW

THEA STILTON: THE CLOUD CASTLE

Check out all my fabumouse adventures!

#1 Lost Treasure of the Emerald Eye   **#2 The Curse of the Cheese Pyramid**   **#3 Cat and Mouse in a Haunted House**   **#4 I'm Too Fond of My Fur!**   **#5 Four Mice Deep in the Jungle**

#6 Paws Off, Cheddarface!   **#7 Red Pizzas for a Blue Count**   **#8 Attack of the Bandit Cats**   **#9 A Fabumouse Vacation for Geronimo**   **#10 All Because of a Cup of Coffee**

#11 It's Halloween, You 'Fraidy Mouse!   **#12 Merry Christmas, Geronimo!**   **#13 The Phantom of the Subway**   **#14 The Temple of the Ruby of Fire**   **#15 The Mona Mousa Code**

#16 A Cheese-Colored Camper   **#17 Watch Your Whiskers, Stilton!**   **#18 Shipwreck on the Pirate Islands**   **#19 My Name Is Stilton, Geronimo Stilton**   **#20 Surf's Up, Geronimo!**

#21 The Wild, Wild West

#22 The Secret of Cacklefur Castle

A Christmas Tale

#23 Valentine's Day Disaster

#24 Field Trip to Niagara Falls

#25 The Search for Sunken Treasure

#26 The Mummy with No Name

#27 The Christmas Toy Factory

#28 Wedding Crasher

#29 Down and Out Down Under

#30 The Mouse Island Marathon

#31 The Mysterious Cheese Thief

Christmas Catastrophe

#32 Valley of the Giant Skeletons

#33 Geronimo and the Gold Medal Mystery

#34 Geronimo Stilton, Secret Agent

#35 A Very Merry Christmas

#36 Geronimo's Valentine

#37 The Race Across America

#38 A Fabumouse School Adventure

#39 Singing Sensation

#40 The Karate Mouse

#41 Mighty Mount Kilimanjaro

#42 The Peculiar Pumpkin Thief

#43 I'm Not a Supermouse!

#44 The Giant
Diamond Robbery

#45 Save the White
Whale!

#46 The Haunted
Castle

#47 Run for the Hills,
Geronimo!

#48 The Mystery in
Venice

#49 The Way of
the Samurai

#50 This Hotel Is
Haunted!

#51 The Enormouse
Pearl Heist

#52 Mouse in Space!

#53 Rumble in
the Jungle

#54 Get into Gear,
Stilton!

#55 The Golden
Statue Plot

#56 Flight of the
Red Bandit

Special Edition!

The Hunt for the
Golden Book

#57 The Stinky
Cheese Vacation

#58 The Super
Chef Contest

#59 Welcome to
Moldy Manor

Special Edition!

The Hunt for the
Curious Cheese

#60 The Treasure of
Easter Island

#61 Mouse House
Hunter

 *Don't miss
my journeys
through time!*

Meet
GERONIMO STILTONOOT

He is a cavemouse—Geronimo Stilton's ancient ancestor! He runs the stone newspaper in the prehistoric village of Old Mouse City. From dealing with dinosaurs to dodging meteorites, his life in the Stone Age is full of adventure!

#1 The Stone of Fire

#2 Watch Your Tail!

#3 Help, I'm in Hot Lava!

#4 The Fast and the Frozen

#5 The Great Mouse Race

#6 Don't Wake the Dinosaur!

#7 I'm a Scaredy-Mouse!

#8 Surfing for Secrets

#9 Get the Scoop, Geronimo!

Don't miss any of these exciting Thea Sisters adventures!

Thea Stilton and the
Dragon's Code

Thea Stilton and the
Mountain of Fire

Thea Stilton and the
Ghost of the Shipwreck

Thea Stilton and the
Secret City

Thea Stilton and the
Mystery in Paris

Thea Stilton and the
Cherry Blossom Adventure

Thea Stilton and the
Star Castaways

Thea Stilton: Big Trouble
in the Big Apple

Thea Stilton and the
Ice Treasure

Thea Stilton and the
Secret of the Old Castle

Thea Stilton and the
Blue Scarab Hunt

Thea Stilton and the
Prince's Emerald

Thea Stilton and the Mystery
on the Orient Express

Thea Stilton and the
Dancing Shadows

Thea Stilton and the
Legend of the Fire Flowers

Thea Stilton and the
Spanish Dance Mission

Thea Stilton and the
Journey to the Lion's Den

Thea Stilton and the
Great Tulip Heist

Thea Stilton and the
Chocolate Sabotage

Thea Stilton and the
Missing Myth

Thea Stilton and the
Lost Letters

Thea Stilton and the
Tropical Treasure

MEET
GERONIMO STILTONIX

He is a spacemouse — the Geronimo Stilton of a parallel universe! He is captain of the spaceship *MouseStar 1*. While flying through the cosmos, he visits distant planets and meets crazy aliens. His adventures are out of this world!

#1 Alien Escape

#2 You're Mine, Captain!

#3 Ice Planet Adventure

#4 The Galactic Goal

#5 Rescue Rebellion

See you on the next journey to the Kingdom of Fantasy!